Born in 1912, **Anthony Buckeridge** was sent to boarding school in Sussex at the age of eight. He went on to university before working as a tutor in a preparatory school and later became a fireman during the Second World War. Buckeridge was the first writer to use prep schools as a setting for his stories and, as such, is the creator of the infamous Jennings. He has written twenty-five 'Jennings' titles in total, which have sold over six million books worldwide, and he was awarded an OBE in the 2003 New Years Honours List. Anthony Buckeridge lives in Sussex with his wife, Eileen.

According to Jennings
Especially Jennings!
Jennings Abounding
Jennings Again!
Jennings As Usual
Jennings At Large
Jennings Follows a Clue
Jennings Goes to School
Jennings In Particular
Jennings, of Course!
The Jennings Report
Jennings' Diary
Jennings' Little Hut
Just Like Jennings
Leave it to Jennings
Our Friend Jennings
Speaking of Jennings
Take Jennings, For Instance
Thanks to Jennings
That's Jennings
The Trouble With Jennings
Trust Jennings!
Typically Jennings

Jennings and Darbishire

HOUSE OF
STRATUS

This edition published in 2003 by House of Stratus, an imprint of
House of Stratus Ltd, Thirsk Industrial Park, York Road, Thirsk,
North Yorkshire, YO7 3BX, UK.

www.houseofstratus.com

Typeset by House of Stratus, printed and bound by Short Run Press Limited.

A catalogue record for this book is available from the British Library
and the Library of Congress.

ISBN 0-7551-0153-7

To
MJS

Contents

1

Happy Returns

For one fleeting moment after he awoke, Jennings lay still, puzzling over the urgent message that was hammering at his sleepy brain and demanding to be let in. Something important had made him wake early: what on earth could it be? Then he remembered. It was his birthday!

His first impulse was to leap out of bed with a joyful "Wacko!" and broadcast the news at full volume to the sleeping dormitory; but second thoughts warned him to wait until the mounds under the neighbouring bedclothes had yawned and stretched themselves into human shape. After all, he reasoned, eleventh birthdays only happen once in a lifetime, and it would be a waste of important news to make the announcement to an audience still drowsy with sleep.

Jennings sat up and glanced at the next bed along the line where Darbishire lay sleeping. Of course, Darbishire was his best friend, and best friends are different. It would hardly be fair, he decided, to let a decent chap like old Darbi snooze away the precious minutes of a red-letter day like this. He must be roused at once!

There was a comfortable, carefree feeling about the friendship between Jennings and Darbishire. It had started when they had met as new boys at Linbury Court Preparatory

School, and had deepened its roots as they had weathered a year of school life together. Yet in appearance and character the two boys were as different as chalk from cheese. Jennings was a lively, impulsive boy with a wide-awake look in his eyes and a briskness about his movements. He had a flair for being in the swim – and some times out of his depth – when any unexpected splash ruffled the smooth waters of boarding school life.

Darbishire's was a less adventurous spirit. Although Nature had never intended him for a man of action, loyalty to Jennings demanded that he should try his best to become one. And try he did, in his own vague and unpractical way.

Very little of Darbishire was visible as he lay asleep that morning. Just a tangle of fair curly hair and the tip of a nose that twitched like a rabbit's, at the ticklish touch of the blanket. From the bed rail above the pillow, a pair of spectacles hung perilously by one earpiece.

"Wake up, Darbishire, wake up!" A hand shook the hunched shoulders and Darbishire opened one eye.

"What's the matter – fire practice?" he demanded sleepily.

"No, you coot. Today's the day! My birthday!"

"Uh? Oh, yes, of course. Wacko! Many happies." And Darbishire closed his eye and turned over to enjoy a few more minutes of refreshing sleep.

"Oh, wake up, Darbi!" Jennings persisted. "If we get dressed in top gear we can get downstairs before the postman comes. It's nearly time for the rising bell."

"It always is time for something before you're ready for it," came in sleepy tones from beneath the blankets. "I reckon they must be making the nights a lot shorter these days. It seems only yesterday that I went to bed."

"Well, so it was! You wouldn't say cootish things like that if you were awake. Buck up and get weaving! I'll race you getting dressed, if you like." As Jennings danced away to the washbasins, his mind's eye conjured up a vision of perspiring postmen pedalling up the drive with parcels of intriguing shape balanced on their handlebars.

He smiled his congratulations at his reflection in the mirror, and a moment later noisy splashings announced that he was celebrating the occasion with a special birthday wash. Two minutes of energetic flannelling and thirty seconds of foaming at the mouth with pink toothpaste, and the ceremony was over.

He turned away from the basin to see Darbishire, still in his pyjamas, practising clove hitches round the bed rail with his dressing-gown cord.

"Oh, for goodness' sake," Jennings protested, "how can we have a race if you go on sitting there?"

"Just coming," Darbishire apologised. "I was only practising my knots."

"What knots?"

"You mean which knots – not what knots. Whatnots are something quite different."

"Different from what?" Jenning demanded.

Darbishire yawned: he was still very sleepy, and this was a difficult question. "I don't know," he confessed. "Different from whichnots, I suppose. Mind you, they're all jolly useful, which-ever sort you do. People often tie knots in things to remind them not to forget things – like, say, for instance, your birthday."

"But you know that already," Jenning argued as he waved his arms into his shirt, "and there's nothing else you've got specially to remember, is there?"

"Oh, yes," Darbishire replied earnestly. "Tying a knot in my dressing-gown cord reminds me that I've got to get up as soon as I've done it."

The rising bell sounded as he spoke, and all along the dormitory heads stirred on pillows and jaws yawned their greeting to the new day. In the beds beyond the washbasins, Venables, Temple and Atkinson came to life and started a lively debate about whether they had had kippers or sausages for breakfast the previous Friday week.

Venables, an untidy boy and tall for his twelve years, was certain it had been kippers, and sought to prove his argument by shouting twice as loudly as the supporters of sausage.

Jennings bore down upon the discussion group.

"I say, I bet you characters don't know what day it is," he began.

"It's Friday," replied Venables. "Just a fortnight since we had kippers for breakfast."

"Ah, yes – but what else?"

"What else? Porridge and bread and marmalade and…"

"No; I mean there's something special about today."

"Sausages for breakfast?" queried Temple hopefully.

"No, you clodpoll. It's my birthday!" And Jennings jumped upon Atkinson and punched him lightly in the ribs, to show that all was well with the world.

"Oh, wacko! Hope you get a decent cake," said Venables.

"Bags I have Atkinson's hunk, if it's marzipan, because he doesn't like it," Temple put in quickly.

"Don't worry. There'll be massive chunks for everybody," Jennings assured them. "My mother's sending me a super-cracking-sonic cake. I'm just hoofing down to the hall now to see if the postman's come."

Gargling strange engine noises from the back of his throat, Jennings raced down the dormitory. As it was a special occasion he decided to be a jet-propelled fighter: he wheeled in and out between the beds, banking steeply and varying the roar of his engine with each sharp turn. He was just going into a power dive to avoid a chest of drawers, when the dormitory door was flung open and the master on duty appeared, without so much as a gale warning to forecast his stormy approach.

"Jennings! Come here!"

The jet fighter switched off its engine and made a forced landing on the runway between two beds. But the damage was already done; for the master on duty was Mr Wilkins and he was eyeing the unhappy aircraft with displeasure.

Mr Wilkins was large and energetic, with a voice and footstep to match his muscular frame. He could be pleasant enough when he chose, but he was not, by nature, a patient man and he could never quite fathom why boys of eleven would neither reason nor behave in the intelligent manner of their elders.

"What on earth were you making that ghastly noise for, Jennings?" he demanded, slamming the door behind him with a crash that made Jennings' engine-gargling sound like the soft whisperings of the wind in the willows. "And why are you dressed already? You know perfectly well you're not allowed out of bed before the rising bell goes."

"Yes, sir: I was in a rather special sort of hurry, with reasons, sir."

Mr Wilkins was not interested in reasons. Curtly, he said: "The rule says, no getting up before the bell. Very well, then, you can stay in during football this afternoon and do some work for me. Now get undressed again and wash properly."

"Yes, sir," said Jennings, and the thrill of the birthday morning seemed suddenly blurred. Why did things like that always have to happen on a day like this? Chaps who had birthdays in the holidays just didn't know how lucky they were.

As he turned sorrowfully away, a sockless Darbishire came slithering along the dormitory and skidded to a halt before the duty master.

"Please, sir! Mr Wilkins, sir!"

"Well, what is it, Darbishire? Hurry up, I'm busy."

"It's his birthday today, sir."

"Oh!" A sudden, almost magical change came over Mr Wilkins; in a moment his impatient frown was gone; his eyebrows, arched in exasperation, dropped to their normal level and the ghost of a smile did its best to haunt the corners of his mouth. Darbishire had found the chink in his armour!

"Oh! Well, if it's his birthday, I suppose we'd better give him another chance. All right, then, Jennings, we won't say any more about it this time."

Mr Wilkins stalked down the dormitory, trying hard to make up for his burst of generosity by barking more brusquely than usual at everybody who was not celebrating a birthday that morning. The fact was that his violent manner concealed a kind heart; its beat was sometimes a little weak, but it was there, and, at odd moments, ready to persuade its owner against his better judgment.

Jennings flashed Darbishire a look of gratitude and murmured: "I thought I'd had it that time. Decent of you to barge in like that."

"That's all right," smiled the benefactor modestly. "You can call it my birthday present to you, if you like. I was a bit worried about not having anything to give you, but now I've dished out this special birthday treat, that let's me out nicely."

"But you haven't given me a treat!"

"I wizard well have! If you don't think stopping Old Wilkie from kicking up a supersonic hoo-ha isn't a decent birthday present, then all I can say is…"

"All right: we won't argue. Buck up and put your socks on and we'll go down and see if the post has come."

Together they left the dormitory and hurried down to the main hall where they found the morning mail stacked on a table.

"Wacko! There's a whole pile of letters for me," Jenning cried excitedly, hopping from one foot to the other. "And three parcels. The big one's my cake and the square fat one's probably Aunt Angela."

Darbishire peered at the parcel, through dusty spectacles. "Don't be crazy; she couldn't be that shape unless she'd been cremated."

"No, you prehistoric ruin! I mean that's good old Aunt Angela's present. And this is my father's writing on the oblong one."

The third parcel was marked *Fragile – with care*. Jennings strained his eyes at the oblong package as though the keenness of his gaze might penetrate the thick brown paper. "What sort of thing would be labelled *Fragile*?"

"Teapots, electric light bulbs, cut-glass vases," hazarded Darbishire helpfully.

"You're bats! What would *I* do with a cut-glass vase?"

"Keep flowers in it."

"But why should my father think I wanted one?"

"I never said he did! You asked me what was fragile and I said…"

"All right; don't let's go through it all over again." Jennings prodded the fragile parcel thoughtfully. "I shall go off pop if I don't find out what it is soon. All I can feel is a wedge of packing."

"Shake it and see if it rattles."

"No wizard fear – it's fragile already. I don't want my parcel going off pop as well as me."

So, in order to avoid the risk of an untimely explosion, they took the parcels along to the tuck-box room and opened them at once.

The large one contained his birthday cake, as he had expected, and it looked so inviting that Darbishire's nail scissors were brought into play and snippets of icing were hacked off and sampled. *JCTJ – Many happy returns* was written on the top in sprawling chocolate letters.

Next came the parcel marked fragile. It was big enough at the start, but as layer upon layer of shavings was removed to litter the floor, it seemed to Jennings that whatever lay within must be shrinking in the most alarming fashion. Frenziedly he hurled out handfuls of tissue paper, as though speed at reaching the middle was the only way to save the contents from disappearing altogether.

At last he got there; and a warmth of happiness spread over him as he lifted his father's present from its nest of wrappings.

"A camera! Gosh, how super-wacko-sonic! It's the one thing I was hoping he wouldn't give me anything else except!" he crowed delightedly, and turned the small object over and over in his hands. "We can do all sorts of things with a camera, can't we, Darbi!"

"We'll bust it, if we do," his friend warned him solemnly. "Much better just to use it for taking photos with."

"That's what I meant. I can take one of you standing up, for instance, and you can take one of me, say, sitting down, and then I can take one of you sitting down and you can take…"

"There's another parcel to open yet."

"Oh yes, of course. Good old Aunt Angela!"

As Jennings tore the wrappings from the last package his eye lighted on a square cardboard box. *The Ideal Junior Printing Outfit* was inscribed on the lid, and below this was pasted an illustrated label showing two boys engaged in printing a highly-coloured magazine on an up-to-date printing machine seldom seen outside Fleet Street. Considering the amount of printer's ink they were using, their fingers were remarkably clean.

The contents of the box, however, were more modest than the label suggested. Raised letters made from small pieces of rubber were neatly arranged in a slotted wooden frame, and a pair of tweezers was provided for removing the type and setting it up in the printing block. The whole thing looked absurdly simple; a quick choice of letters, a slick jab at the ink pad, and the thought behind the printed word was inscribed for ever in a vivid mauve hue.

"Jolly good!" said Darbishire. "We can print our names on all our private possessions, and stick up notices, like, say, *Keep Out,* or *Venables is a clodpoll!*"

But Jennings' ideas were more ambitious. "The first thing I'm going to use it for is to answer all these birthday letters," he announced. "It'll save masses of time because I always write the same thing to everyone, anyway."

With extreme care, Darbishire removed a row of letters from the box and held them with the tweezers. He peered at them closely, for his spectacles still bore the previous day's film of dust and gave a blurred, frosted-glass appearance to everything in sight.

"I can't make out whether these are *e*'s or *a*'s," he said doubtfully. "My father says that in the olden days they used to…"

But at that moment he squeezed too hard with the tweezers; the little rubber pellets shot from between the prongs and catapulted through the air to the four corners of the room.

"You clumsy bazooka!" Jennings said heatedly. "We'll have a frantic job to find them with all these shavings about."

"Super sorrow; they were a bit slippery."

On hands and knees they began the search among the piles of shavings and the yawning cracks between the floorboards, but the breakfast bell sounded before so much as a single rubber pellet had come to light.

"Oh fish-hooks, what are we going to do?" lamented Darbishire. "All those letters I lost were the same sort. We'll be up a gum tree if we don't find them."

A quick glance in the box showed that Darbishire was right. The letters were arranged alphabetically – a batch of *a*'s, the same number of *b*'s, then *c*'s and *d*'s…and then came the gap. There wasn't an *e* in the box!

"We'll come back and have another squint after breakfast," Jennings decided, as he put his presents in his tuck box. "We're bound to find them then."

But after breakfast was too late. When the boys returned, they found that Robinson, the odd-job man, had been busy. The room had been tidied, the shavings removed: dust, rubbish and stray rubber pellets had all been swallowed up by the vacuum cleaner.

For some moments they stood staring at the orderly rows of tuck-boxes. Then Jennings turned and led the way upstairs to the common room.

"Well, this *has* bashed things up," he complained bitterly. "How am I going to write my birthday 'thank you' letters now?"

"Perhaps you could think of something to say that doesn't need any *e*'s" suggested Darbishire.

"Huh! You try, if you're so clever. Besides I had a supersonic idea during breakfast about something we could do during hobbies' hour next week. I've finished my clay modelling and Mr Wilkins gets in a frantic bate if you just swing about on the desks and say you haven't got anything to do."

"You mean we could stick up our *Keep Out* notices and things?"

Jennings looked scornful. "No, something a wizard sight better. I vote, why not let's start a Form Three specially printed magazine. I could be chief editor and you could be the office boy or a journalist or something. We could get hold of all the latest news, print it on my outfit and then stick it up on the noticeboard."

"Gosh, yes: super-wacko wheeze!" In a sudden flash of imagination Darbishire saw himself as the bustling eagle-eyed crime reporter, pounding along on the trail of sensational scoops. "Who's that?" people were saying, as he raced along vague, unspecified streets. "Why, don't you know! That's C E J Darbishire, ace news-sleuth of the Form Three newspaper. He's quite a legend in stop-press circles."

Then the little dream faded, and more seriously he turned to Jennings and said: "Yes, but it's going to be jolly awkward if we can't print any news that's got an *e* in it."

"That's all right. I'll ask Aunt Angela for some spares. And while we're waiting for them we can plan out what sort of things we're going to print."

Jennings was so pleased with his idea that he went on thinking about it for the rest of the morning. In fact, it was in the middle of Mr Wilkins' algebra class after break that he conceived the brilliant idea of appointing himself chief press-photographer. He wondered why he hadn't thought of it before. After all, every decent magazine illustrated its columns with photographs, and here was he with a brand new camera just asking to be made use of! He made a note on his algebra book to raise this topic at the editorial conference called for the following week, and then set about the business of enjoying his birthday to the full.

It was a good birthday, too, considering that it came during term time; and the kind Fate that looks after people on these occasions rallied round and did what it could to help. It provided his favourite pudding at lunch time, and saw to it that there was enough for a second helping; it allowed him to find his best form during football that afternoon, so that he scored two goals and walked off the field feeling right up on top of the world. And finally, the kind Fate persuaded Venables and Atkinson to borrow eleven torch bulbs and a supply of batteries, and spend the half hour before tea wiring them to Jennings' birthday cake to compensate for its lack of candles.

The illuminations were a great success, and actually stayed alight for short periods when no one happened to be jogging the table.

After tea that evening, Jennings settled down in the common room to answer his birthday letters. He was anxious to try out his printing set on something fairly simple to start with, so that he might master any unexpected snags before starting on the more difficult task of coping with a magazine.

Patiently he set up the type; the missing e's were rather a problem and he had to substitute x's in their place, which gave the correspondence a secret, code-like appearance. His first attempts were a failure because so many of the letters seemed to turn themselves upside-down, or decided to face the wrong way, in spite of the compositor's most careful attention. But he persevered, and when Darbishire burst into the common room half an hour later, Jennings was able to show him the results of his labours.

"It works wizardly, Darbi," he greeted him. "Come and have a look. All I've got to do now is…"

"Yes, but hang on a minute; I've got something to tell you," Darbishire began.

"Never mind other things now. What do you think about this?"

"I was only going to say…"

Jennings thrust the top sheet of paper into Darbishire's hands, and was too wrapped up in his own triumph to notice that the hands were dirtier than they should have been, and that his friend's whole appearance suggested that he had just finished a hard day's work in a corporation rubbish dump.

"Not bad, is it!" Jennings said proudly. "Of course, we'll have to wait for those *e*'s before we get cracking on the mag."

Darbishire postponed his explanations and read the sheet of paper held before his nose.

"Dxar…" the circular began.

"I hopx you arx quitx wxll. I likxd thx birthday prxsxnts I had vxry much indxxd. Dad sxnt mx a camxra and Darbishirx gavx mx a spxcial trxat…"

Darbishire broke off his reading and said: "Well, I know what you mean, of course, but if you listen to what…"

"If you're worrying about the *x*'s, you needn't because I've put a special PS on Aunt Angela's letter. It's a bit tricky asking for something when you haven't got any to explain with, but I expect she'll understand."

Aunt Angela's postscript read:

"Plxasx sxnd mx somx morx of thx lxttxrs that comx bxtwxxn *d* and *f*."

As he finished reading it, Darbishire fished in his pocket and produced a small handful of rubber pellets.

"Here you are," he said as he put them on the desk. "These are the *e*'s I lost this morning."

"What?"

"Yes, I've spent the last half-hour scrounging through the dustbag on the vacuum cleaner. You can do all your birthday thank you letters again properly, now."

"No wizard fear!" returned Jennings firmly. "We've got to get on with our magazine, and there's a lot more in that than just setting up the type and sitting back and twiddling your thumbs. We've got to get hold of the latest news and take photos of it and...and, well, that may sound easy to you, but all sorts of things can happen, and perhaps even one or two things might go wrong before we get the hang of a super important job like this."

Jennings never spoke a truer word! But even so, he had no idea of just *what* could happen, or *how* wrong things could go!

2

The Unwelcome Gift

It was generally agreed that the hobbies hour was the most popular item on the timetable. It was held on Mondays during the Christmas term, and an added delight was that it took the place of evening preparation.

The Headmaster, Mr Pemberton-Oakes, had decreed that the hour should be used for creative activities and, accordingly, he expected a quiet and restrained atmosphere to prevail.

In this, he was unlucky; for few boys can create quietly when their tools are hammer and saw, and there is something about paint and glue, strip metal and balsa wood, which plays havoc with a restrained atmosphere.

There was, therefore a purposeful bustle in the hobbies room after tea on the following Monday. Venables and Temple were modelling an African landscape on a sheet of corrugated iron: large lumps of coke, tinted with poster paint, formed rocky mountain slopes where plasticine elephants stalked amongst an undergrowth of twigs and shavings. It was a convincing jungle scene – apart from a miniature telephone kiosk and three polar bears in the north-west corner.

Atkinson was constructing a patchwork Red Indian wigwam from snippets of grey flannel and darning wool which he had borrowed from the sewing-room. Bromwich was hard at work on a rabbit-hutch; he had no rabbit and no hope of ever possessing one, but as a hutch was the next best thing he was determined to make a good one.

It was in this hive of creative activity that Jennings and Darbishire settled down, with notebook and pencil, to their editorial conference. They sat at a table between Thompson, who was making a puppet, and Binns, who was making a great deal of noise.

"Now, first of all, Darbi, we've got to think of a name for our magazine," Jennings began. "So I vote, what about calling it the *Form Three Times*?"

"Not long enough," objected Darbishire. "Most decent papers always have a whole chunk more, like, say for instance, '*with which is incorporated the Lower Hockleton and District Illustrated Mercury and Weekly Advertiser.*' "

"Huh! They wouldn't say all that if they only had a titchy little rubber printing outfit to do it with. The less we start incorporating the better, until we've got the hang of things." Jennings glanced at the agenda in his notebook. "Now, by rights, I ought to be chief editor because it's my printing outfit, but I don't mind putting it to the vote, just to be fair."

Darbishire's eyes brightened behind his spectacles: he would dearly have liked to be chief editor.

"Wacko!" he agreed. "But I vote we're not allowed to vote for ourselves because my father says it's swanking to blow your own trumpet."

"All right, then. I'll blow your trumpet, if you blow mine. Here's a bit of paper to write your vote on."

The ballot resulted in a tie, each candidate polling one vote, and the deadlock was finally solved by the toss of a coin. Jennings was appointed editor with Darbishire as his chief assistant. There were other vacancies to be filled, and the editor lost no time in filling them. "You can be chief Special

Correspondent and Gardening expert as well, Darbi, and I'll be chief Sports Reporter and Press-Photographer."

"Couldn't we swap? I'd much rather be the Sports Reporter."

The editor looked reprovingly at his staff. "You're crackers!" he said. "You know wizard well you play football like a left-footed sparrow. Who on earth would want to read what *you* wrote?"

The Chief Special Correspondent sighed. He knew this was only too true. "Well, couldn't I write under a *nom de plume*? Then no one would know it was me."

"Write under a *what*?"

"A *nom de plume*. It means a pen name. I could call myself Half-time Henry or Touchline Timothy or something."

"You can't possibly have a pen name, because we shan't be using pens. Of course, you could have a *nom de printing outfit* if you're all that keen on it."

The discussion went forward at a brisk pace. Soon they had decided that the first number of the *Form Three Times* should appear towards the end of the following week. It was to be printed on single sheets of paper, and limited to one copy, posted on the common room noticeboard.

Their voices grew louder as their plans progressed; and as the news of their venture spread across the room, the space round the editor's table became thronged with elbow-jogging helpers anxious to contribute news items for publication.

Binns had the shrillest voice in the room and trumpeted his announcement into the editor's ear in a series of nerve-racking shrieks.

"If you bods want a basinful of really smashing news, you can come to me for it. Honestly, Jennings, I'm not pulling your leg. There's been a Mysterious Disappearance!"

"Who's vanished – Mr Wilkins?" inquired Darbishire hopefully.

"No: my left football boot's been stolen out of my locker. And if you want to know what I think, I shouldn't be surprised if there's been an organised gangster on the job, because I've worked out how he could have done it. He could have left his car on the quad while we were all in class and…"

"Don't be so bats, Binns! Why should anyone want to pinch just one boot?"

"He might have been a chap with only one leg."

"He'd have a bit of a job playing football, then, wouldn't he?"

Binns minor hadn't thought of that, and by the time he had worked out a convincing answer, the editor's ear was busy with an exclusive news scoop from Temple about a threatened detention class.

There was no shortage of news, but it was not *new* news, and when the throng of elbow-joggers and shoulder-tappers had thinned, Jennings faced the fact squarely.

"What we've got to do, Darbi, is to get going with the camera," he decided. "If we can get some decent action photos it may liven things up a bit."

"Righto! We could start tomorrow, if the sun's out. You can take a photo of me, sitting down, and I can take one of you standing up and…"

"Gosh, no; that's no earthly use. Who wants to see your face plastered all over the wall? What we want is something like the winning goal in the Cup Final, or jet fighters zooming into a power dive."

"Or the semi-final of the Form Four chess championship."

"Yes, that's the idea – plenty of action. We might go down to the harbour and get a photo of a battleship or…"

"You're crazy," interposed his assistant. "You couldn't get a battleship into Linbury Cove. There's only a titchy little wooden jetty, and anything bigger than something quite small would get stuck in the entrance."

"All the better if it *did* get stuck – it'd make a smashing photo. I vote we ask permish to go next Sunday, when we're out for our walks. Then we can develop it in time for the first edition."

The more Jennings thought about the photographic expedition, the better he liked it: it would bring a breath of the outside world into the narrow limits of boarding school life and stamp the *Form Three Times* as an up-to-date paper whose roving press-photographer kept a finger on the pulse of the world's affairs. But it would be some days before the boys could obtain permission to leave the grounds, so they spent the intervening time searching for items of news.

They had unearthed the sensational story of how Atkinson had found a caterpillar in his cabbage; but as it had happened the term before last, they felt that this could hardly be headlined as late news. As chief Crime Reporter, Jennings compiled a list of the defaulters in Mr Wilkins' detention class, with details of their misdeeds and a brief note about their previous convictions. And Darbishire, to his great delight, secured a scoop by being on the scene when Bromwich broke the Dormitory 6 breath-holding record by staying under the bath water for a count of thirty-eight.

Sunday seemed a long time coming round that week, and when at last it did arrive, it was a wet one; but after lunch the weather cleared slightly – and the boys lost no time in handing their names to Mr Carter, the senior master. Then, armed with the camera and shrouded in raincoats, they hurried along the downland paths which led through Linbury village to the sea.

"This is super, isn't it!" said Jennings, as the harbour came in sight. "If we can get a decent photo for the front page…" He broke off and hopped up and down in triumph. "Oh, wacko, Darbi, we *can!* I can see the mast of a ship tied up to the jetty."

"Battleship?" inquired Darbishire, but without much hope. He removed his drizzle-spotted glasses and wiped them on the sleeve of his raincoat.

"No; it's a fishing boat. Let's go and have a squint at zero feet."

The rain had stopped now, and a watery sun was doing its best to pierce the grey clouds as the two boys slithered and skidded down the wet chalky path to the shore.

It would be stretching the facts to say that Linbury Cove was a harbour, although a wooden jetty stretched out from the shingly beach, and here yachts and small craft were occasionally moored and fishing boats took shelter when the Channel was rough. There was only one boat at its moorings that afternoon – a fishing vessel with its port of origin painted on the stern in yellow letters.

"Golly, it's French," exclaimed Jennings in surprise. "It's got Boulogne on the back."

Darbishire looked slightly shocked. "You are an ignorant bazooka, Jen; you ought to know ships don't have backs. You mean it's got its name abaft."

"Well, it's French, anyway."

"Abaft isn't French. It's English for the wide end of the boat. But what I can't understand is what it's doing here at all."

Darbishire's surprise was natural, for it was not often that anything but local craft put into Linbury Cove: but the Channel had been squally on the previous night and the *Sainte Marie*, fishing far from home, had been only too ready to seek refuge in the bay. Soon the weather would be calm enough to put to sea again, but for the moment the five members of the crew were content to sit about on the deck, mending their nets and peeling potatoes.

Jennings took two snaps of the stern; one with his finger over the lens and one without. Then he said: "I wonder if they'd let us go aboard and take them in a group?"

"We could ask them; they might even pose for us. I say, won't everyone at school get a shock when they see the French fishing fleet all over page one!"

"It'll be a bit of a shock for the camera, too," said Jennings. "I've never seen such a plug-ugly bunch of characters in my life."

There was some truth in this remark, for the crew of the *Sainte Marie*, in their working clothes, would have won no prizes at a fashion show. All five wore greasy blue overalls, faded and stained to such an extent that it was impossible to distinguish the patches of oil from the patches of blue cloth which seemed to be all that held the garments together. Their seamen's caps were shapeless with age and their ancient sea-boots flapped in folds about their ankles. They were tough, wiry men with weather-beaten features, stubbly chins and – as it turned out – hearts of gold.

"Well, it's no good just standing and looking at them." Darbishire observed. "My father says you should strike while the iron is hot, and faint heart never won fair lady."

"I'm not striking anyone with hot irons, whatever your father says; and I don't want a fair lady – I want a photo of a fisherman."

"Go on, then; ask them. I dare you to."

Jennings favoured his assistant with a superior smile.

Little things like this were all in the day's work for a keen press-photographer. Politely, he called:

"Er – excuse me; just for a moment, I say!"

There was no answer from the boat, where five pairs of hands toiled amongst tarred netting and potato peel. Jennings

21

tried again – louder this time. "Ahoy there! Attention all shipping!"

The hands stopped work; five oily peaked caps swivelled round and five whiskery chins were tilted upwards towards the jetty.

"Excuse me," Jennings repeated, "but my friend and I were wondering whether you'd mind frightfully if we came on board and took a snap of you for our mag."

No answer. Puzzled stares greeted the polite inquiry, and after ten seconds of embarrassing silence Jennings felt that more explanation was called for. "What I mean is, we thought you'd make a supersonic picture just sitting there and messing about with those nets."

"*Comment?*" It was the smallest of the Frenchmen who spoke; a thin, dark-haired man with beetling brows and a chin like emery paper.

"What did he say?" whispered Darbishire.

"I'm not sure. It sounded like 'come on!'"

"I know it did, but I think he really said *comment*. That means how many, or what, or something in French. At least, I think it does."

"I only want to take one photo. I'd better tell him." And raising his voice Jennings called: "One will be enough, thank you."

The little fisherman looked helplessly at his equally bewildered colleagues. "*Comment?*" he inquired again

But things were no clearer up on the jetty. "It can't mean *how many* because I've just told him that, and now he's asked again. Perhaps he does mean *come on*. Let's go, anyway."

An iron ladder stretched from the jetty to the craft below. Jennings led the way and a few moments later the boys had scrambled over the gunwhale onto the deck.

Seen at close quarters, the *Sainte Marie* was picturesque, but untidy; tangled coils of rope lay ready to trip the unwary foot; loaves of bread and tins of engine oil lay side by side on the deck, and everywhere there was a strong pervasive smell of raw fish.

The fishermen smiled and nodded at their visitors; but they said nothing, for the very good reason that they spoke English no better than the boys spoke French. Jennings felt that it was up to him to establish friendly relations. "Good afternoon; it's jolly decent of you to invite us on board," he began.

"*Comment?*" This time the speaker was a twinkling-eyed man with tiny gold earrings.

"We can't *come on* any more – we're abaft already," Darbishire explained. But the expressions on his hosts' faces remained blank and he turned to Jennings in despair.

"This is hopeless, Jen. They just don't understand English."

"Perhaps they would if I spoke a bit louder." And this time he shouted at the top of his voice: "Please – can – I – take – your – photos?"

For one second the fishermen stared blankly and then, all together, they burst into a torrent of rapid idiomatic French with wavings of oily fingers and shruggings of eloquent shoulders. Jennings and Darbishire stood and listened and understood not one word of the stream of sound that was cascading about their ears. Suddenly it stopped.

"*Comment?*" queried Jennings brightly. He knew he was safe in saying that.

The twinkling-eyed man laid a hand on his shoulder. "*Nous ne comprenons pas: sommes français. Nous ne parlons pas anglais du tout.*"

"He says they don't speak English," interpreted Darbishire. "You'll have to talk to them in French if you want that photo."

"Who, me? No wizard fear," replied Jennings. "You're tons better at it than I am. You were fifth in French last term and I was only two from bottom."

"Yes, but that doesn't mean to say…"

"Oh, go on, Darbi; don't be feeble. I tell you what – I'll appoint you Special Foreign Correspondent to the *Form Three Times*."

Darbishire was delighted with his new appointment, but appalled at the responsibility that went with it. How on earth should he begin? The only French sentence he could call to mind was a passage which had caused him some trouble in class the previous day. So far as he had been able to judge, the translation was: *The gentleman who wears one green hat approaches himself all of a sudden.* Somehow this did not seem a promising way of starting a conversation about photography.

"Just ask if we can take their photo," Jennings urged.

"I couldn't; it'd mean using irregular verbs. They only come at the end of the book, and if these chaps haven't had a very good education they might not have got up to them yet. Give me a bit longer; I'll think of something."

While Darbishire was thinking, Jennings tried mime. He pointed the camera at the fishermen and smiled; but instead of posing, the crew clustered round under the impression that they were being invited to make an inspection at close quarters.

The small dark man poked a finger at the lens. "*Qu'est-ce-que c'est?*" he inquired with interest.

Jennings looked appealingly at the interpreter. "What did he say, Darbi?"

"Well, actually, *qu'est-ce-que c'est* means 'what is this that this is,' if you follow me, but what I think he's trying to ask…"

"Oh, this is hopeless! Surely you can tell them that we want a fisherman to pose for a photo!"

"I'll have a bash," the Foreign Correspondent agreed. In his mind he ran through the present tense of the appropriate verb. Then he cleared his throat and announced: "*Attention mes braves! Nous voulons du Poisson*...er, no, hang on a sec – that's not quite right. What I mean is..."

But a sudden wave of understanding had spread over the faces of the crew now that their visitors' purpose was clear.

"Ah! *Vous voulez du poisson. Attendez!*" And with one accord they turned and hurried down into the hold of the boat.

Jennings watched them in surprise. "Where are they all beetling off to?" he demanded.

The interpreter avoided his friend's eye. "Well, I'm afraid I made a bit of a bish," he confessed. "I couldn't think of the word for 'fisherman' and in the heat of the moment I said *poisson*, which means fish."

"You mean you called them a bunch of fish and they've got insulted and ankled off?"

"No I think I said we *want* some fish."

Jennings clicked his tongue reproachfully. "Well you're a smashing Foreign Correspondent, I must say! Fifth in French last term and you can't even chat with a few old geezers who probably haven't even looked at a French grammar book since they left school."

Darbishire sighed: being an interpreter was not as easy as it sounded.

"Never mind," Jennings consoled him. "I've got a supersonic photo for the front page. They don't know I took it because they were all listening to you telling them they were a bunch of fish, but it should be pretty decent if it comes out."

Darbishire's spirits rose again. "Goodo! We'd better beetle off home then. I'm glad it's over; the strain of talking in a foreign tongue was beginning to tell on me."

They turned to go, but before they had reached the ladder they were stopped by hoarse cries from the open hatchway. Then, one after another, the five members of the crew emerged on deck bearing gifts of plaice, mackerel and cod.

Smiles shone through the grime on the fishermen's faces; for had they not triumphed over the barrier of language to fulfil the wishes of their guests? They advanced upon the boys with hands outstretched, and each hand held a scaly gift.

Jennings backed away in alarm. "Oh, golly, they're not for us, are they – I hope!" But from the encouraging smiles of the donors, it was only too obvious that they were.

"Thanks very much; er – *merci beaucoup* and all that, but we couldn't possibly…"

"*C'est pour votre maman – vous comprenez?*" explained the man with the beetling brows. And then, with great mental effort he sought to make his meaning clear in English. "You geef ze feesh at your mozzer for ze soup."

Jennings looked blank. "I don't think I've got a mozzer to give it at," he faltered.

"*Comment?*"

"What he means is, we've got to take the fish home to our mothers," Darbishire interpreted.

"Tell him you don't have mothers at boarding school; say we're super grateful for the offer, but the deal's off."

"I couldn't possibly. There's too many irregular verbs. Let's take the fish and get weaving – it's the easiest way out."

"But we don't want the wretched stuff. What could we do with them?"

"That's not the point," Darbishire insisted. "They're a present. They think we came on board specially to ask for them and they'll be as upset as two coots if we don't take them with us."

There was nothing for it but to follow Darbishire's advice. Gingerly, Jennings held out his hand and took the unwelcome gift. Then the rest of the fishermen hurried forward with their offerings, which the boys accepted with strained smiles.

To climb the ladder with their slippery burdens was out of the question, and for a moment Jennings hoped that this might prove an excuse for leaving their presents behind. But no! The beetle-browed fisherman unearthed a sheet of newspaper from under a pile of netting and made up a clumsy parcel.

A salvo of friendly farewells followed the boys up the ladder and along the jetty. And this was only natural, for the crew of the *Sainte Marie* were warm-hearted men who took pleasure in performing little acts of kindness.

3

Continental Breakfast

As soon as the boys were well away from the *Sante Marie* Jennings lost no time in criticising the crew's little act of kindness. And most of the blame fell upon the Special Foreign Correspondent.

"You great, prehistoric clodpoll, Darbi," he complained, as he led the way up the cliff path. "What did you want to go and make a frantic bish like that for? It's all very well not wanting to offend them, but we can't cart this parcel back to school with us."

"Why not? There's no rule about it, is there?"

"There's bound to be. Raw fish probably counts as tuck, and Matron would get into a ghastly bate if we marched into tea with them. And even if there isn't a rule, they'd soon make one up. Rule number nine million and forty-seven: 'Any boy beetling into class with twelve slippery raw fish shall hereby be liable to be detained during Mr Wilkins' pleasure.'"

It was clear that difficulties lay ahead and it seemed to Jennings that their best course would be to dispose of the parcel before they reached the school gates. But this was not so easy as it sounded. There was little cover on the open downland, and to make matters worse a middle-aged woman with a fox terrier was walking along the track a few yards behind them. Surely she would think it odd if finny gifts were strewn in her path; and no attempt at concealment would deceive the terrier, who was even now sniffing round Jennings' heels with an inquisitive air.

"We can't dump them now, or she'll probably report us for wasting food, or cruelty to dumb friends or something," Jennings decided. They would have to wait until the woman was out of sight and then... But why should they? A foolproof idea flashed into Jennings' mind; an idea so simple, yet so attractive that it was worth taking a few risks in the carrying out.

"I tell you what, Darbi," he went on, "we'll fox them back to school with us and smuggle them down to my tuck-box."

"Righto, then! And we can take them home to our mothers at the end of term as the man told us to."

Jennings gave his friend a pitying look. "You may think yourself a supersonic interpreter, Darbi, but you've got about as much brains as this fish. Can you imagine what they'd be *like* in about eight weeks' time?"

"I see what you mean," replied Darbishire thoughtfully, "but in that case what's the point of smuggling them back with us?"

"To eat, of course."

"What – raw! Dash it all, Jen, I'm not a sea lion."

As they followed the footpath back to Linbury, Jennings explained his plan. They would rise early the following morning and develop his film in the school dark room, as camera-owners were encouraged to do. Then, safely behind the bolted dark room door, they could fry a tasty fish breakfast over the gas-bracket on the wall. Kitchenware could be improvised from developing dishes, and the problem of finding a substitute for cooking fat could lie solved with a little serious thought.

Darbishire's eyes lit up with excitement. Here was a scheme with no snags attached to it, and the mark of genius lay in the fact that, once inside the dark room no one, not even a master, would think of demanding admission for fear of spoiling the film.

"Oh, wacko, Jennings; jolly good idea – *bon idée!*" Darbishire stopped short, surprised at his ready command of the French language. "Gosh, did you hear what I said then? *Bon idée!* There you are, you see! My French is masses better already, just from having a little informal chat with a few natives."

"Those chaps weren't natives – they were Frenchmen," Jennings returned curtly. "Natives don't speak French; they say things like *wallah-wallah* and *m'bongo-m'bongo.*"

"No; you're thinking of Africans. Our fishermen-geezers were natives of France, so of course they spoke French. Everyone's a native really – even us."

"I'm not; I don't speak French."

"But you don't *have* to. Don't you see…" The pointless argument rambled on until the boys were within sight of the school gates. Then Jennings became alert; the utmost caution was necessary if his plan was to succeed.

He sent Darbishire ahead to make sure that there was no one about on the drive; then, as his arms were cramped from carrying the parcel, he laid it on the ground. It would have to be re-wrapped before it could be carried indoors, he decided, for it had never been a tidy parcel, and now the newspaper was sodden and clammy.

He had just started on this task when Darbishire came hurrying out of the school gates. Alarm and despondency were written all over his features.

"Mr Carter!" he gasped in a voiceless whisper. "He's coming down the drive!"

Hastily Jennings gathered up the parcel. His intention was to conceal it beneath his raincoat, but as he lifted it from the ground the sheet of newspaper dissolved in pulp and the scaly contents cascaded onto the road with a soft, depressing slither.

For a moment Jennings stared at the burst parcel in dismay. Then, quickly, he stooped and began stuffing the tell-tale evidence into his raincoat pockets.

Darbishire's expression registered distaste.

"They'll make a super-chronic mess," he observed.

"Can't help that! If Mr Carter sees them, bang goes my famous wheeze. Come on, don't just stand there, like the back of a bus queue; he'll be round the corner in half a mo."

Unwillingly, Darbishire helped in the task and in a matter of seconds the boys' pockets were bulging to bursting point, and Jennings was looking round desperately for some place to conceal the last fish for which neither of them could find room.

At that moment the scrunch of Mr Carter's footsteps was heard turning the corner of the drive. Jennings took the only course which remained open; snatching off his cap, he laid the last small mackerel inside and then replaced his headgear with feverish haste.

The cap had never been a good fit, and now it perched high up on top of his head like a carnival novelty. It was a makeshift move, but it would have to suffice, for the master was approaching now.

Mr Carter was a friendly-looking man who had reached the comfortable years between youth and middle age. He was quiet and unexcitable – a man whom all the boys liked and turned to in their troubles. He had only one serious failing, so far as the boys were concerned, and this was that however skilfully a wrong-doer might conceal his misdeeds, Mr Carter always found out!

31

"Good afternoon, sir," said Darbishire politely and raised his cap with a courtly flourish: Jennings dared do no more than tweak the peak and pray that Mr Carter would stop staring in that marked manner.

"Good afternoon. You're back early. Did you have a successful expedition?" Mr Carter inquired.

"Yes thank, you, sir. We went to the harbour." Jennings hoped that his voice did not betray his anxiety. Perhaps if he chatted quite naturally the master would not notice anything was amiss. "I took a jolly good photo of the abaft end of a boat, sir, and another one of a group of natives. At least, that's what Darbishire says they were, but they were practically white, really, sir."

If only Mr Carter would not continue to stare like that! Surely he did not suspect anything! Darbishire took up the tale in an effort to divert attention from the bulging cap.

"They weren't really natives, sir – they were aliens, but I found I knew their lingo fairly well, so I was able to have quite a little chat with them, sir."

This was too much for Jennings. Even at the risk of inviting Mr Carter's stare again, he could not let the Special Correspondent claim his miserable failure as a triumph.

"Darbishire's just swanking, sir," he interposed. "They were Frenchmen, and he told them they were a bunch of fish."

"That must have been very comforting for them," said Mr Carter. "There's nothing like a friendly word to make a foreigner feel at home in a strange land."

"Oh, sir, I *didn't* call them that, sir! Jennings' French was so mouldy that he couldn't follow what I was talking about."

"And could the Frenchmen?" inquired Mr Carter.

"Well, yes and no, sir. They said a lot of things very fast that weren't in the grammar book, but I don't think their French was very good really. They hardly used the list of pronoun objects and things at all, sir."

Mr Carter took a deep breath and said: "The first thing you two boys can do, is to go and empty your pockets. Fish may be good for the brain, Jennings, but it should never be applied externally."

So Mr Carter *did* know! It just didn't seem possible to keep anything from him.

"I'm sorry, sir," Jennings apologised. "They were a present, you see. We didn't really want them but we didn't know enough French to explain properly."

"I see. Well, I suggest you dispose of it, and the sooner the better, considering that it's been mixed with whatever rubbish you normally carry in your raincoat pockets. After that, Jennings, you can hang your coats out to air and then wash your hair."

"Yes, sir."

Deflated in spirit, the members of the photographic expedition wended their way up the drive. But by the time they had reached the quad Jennings was feeling more cheerful. After all, they still had the photographs, and matters would have been much worse if Mr Carter had decided to punish them.

Darbishire, however, was still wrapped in gloom. He had been looking forward to that early breakfast.

"What ghastly feeble luck," he lamented. "It's always the same whenever we get a really first class idea."

"I don't see that we've got much to moan about," Jennings replied, as they turned into the main building. "We've still got to develop the photos and then – well, Mr Carter didn't say we *weren't* to eat them, did he?"

"The photos?"

"No, you clodpoll. Why don't you listen properly!"

"But Mr Carter said…"

"He didn't say anything of the sort. He just told us to *dispose* of them; and the best way to do that is fried, with pepper and salt, if you can get some. We can empty our pockets, as he told us to, and put the fish in my tuck-box. After all, I'm sure he didn't really mean we were to waste it."

Jennings and Darbishire spent the rest of the time before tea in making preparations for the morrow. First it was necessary to obtain permission to use the dark room. They decided that it would be wiser not to ask Mr Carter, so they sought out Mr Hind, a studious man with a tired voice, who taught History in the lower forms. Mr Hind gave his permission freely; he was a keen photographer and only too pleased to encourage the boys in their hobby.

The next requirement was a supply of cooking fat. Jennings unearthed a bottle of cricket bat oil, left over from the summer term, but after some argument they decided that this might be lacking in vitamins, so they ate dry bread at tea time and smuggled their pots of butter out of the dining-hall in an envelope. So far, so good; whichever way they looked at it, the scheme seemed flawless.

It was nearly seven o'clock when Jennings slipped out of bed the next morning and shook the sleeping Darbishire into wakefulness. There was a risk, of course, in rising before the bell, but risks have to be faced when important issues are at stake.

Darbishire, however, thought otherwise. The weather was bleak and uninviting; his bed was warm and comfortable, and the idea of filleting raw plaice in a cold dark room did not seem nearly so attractive as it had done the night before.

"Couldn't we do it some other time? One day next week, say," he suggested.

"No, we jolly well couldn't; the fish won't keep. It's highly fragile, don't forget."

"You mean perishable; it was your camera that was fragile and my father says that you should never..."

"Never mind what your father says. I shall be perishable if you keep me hanging about on this cold lino much longer. I'm pretty well perished already."

It was useless to argue and Darbishire knew it. Still bleary with sleep, he crawled out of bed and felt vaguely about for his socks.

As soon as the boys were dressed they tiptoed out of the dormitory, to the accompaniment of a piercing squeak from Jennings' house shoes. They called at the tuck-box room for the fish, now re-wrapped in a strong brown paper bag, and then made for the dark room with as much speed and as little noise as they could.

Darbishire heaved a sigh of relief as he bolted the door. "Phew! Thank goodness we didn't meet anyone in the corridor. Which shall we do first – cook or develop?"

"I've done the developing," Jennings answered, to his friend's surprise. "I came in last night just before the dorm bell went, so's we could have more time to get cracking with our famous breakfast."

"Oh, wizzo! Have they come out all right?"

"Not too mouldy! The fishing ones are super, but I kept forgetting to wind the film on when I took the earlier ones and I've got a snap of Venables saving a goal all mixed up with the back view of Mr Wilkins' head taken through the library window."

This was not the time, however, to examine the photographs, for more immediate tasks were waiting to be done. Jennings picked up a celluloid developing dish and rinsed it out at the little sink in the corner. It would never do for the well-cooked breakfast to taste of hypo! Then he produced the butter from his pocket and four plaice of medium size from the parcel.

Darbishire watched spellbound. Now that things were going smoothly he was beginning to enjoy himself. And what added to his pleasure was the thought that as the fare had been provided by Frenchmen, they could boast to their friends of enjoying a genuine continental breakfast.

"This cookery stunt of yours was a massive brainwave, Jen," he said admiringly. "We should have been up a gumtree otherwise, because if we couldn't have eaten it, it'd just be what my father calls a white elephant, wouldn't it?"

Jennings looked up from his preparations. "What'd be a white elephant?"

"This fish would."

"Listen, Darbi, I've got quite enough trouble cooking fish without starting on white elephants as well."

"I wasn't asking you to. You couldn't cook a white elephant really, because there's no such thing."

"You said there was. You said our fish was one."

"Ah, but what I meant was…"

"If you want to be useful, Darbishire, you can wizard well stop flattering about elephants and shut the window. Anyone about on the quad will know we're not developing a film if we haven't got the black-out up."

The window panes were coated with black paint to exclude the light. Darbishire closed the window and at once the little room grew dark. Jennings groped his way round the table and found the box of matches which was used for lighting the stub of candle in the red dark room lamp. He had, by this time, placed the butter in the developing dish, so all that remained to be done was to light the gas jet and hold the dish over the flame until the butter melted.

He lit the gas. He held the dish over the flame. And then it happened!

There was a sudden flash and tongues of flame were licking the sides of the dish and leaping towards the ceiling.

Jennings said: "Oh, gosh!" and dropped the dish on the floor.

"Help! What's up?" gasped Darbishire in alarm. "Look out, Jen, or you'll set the place on fire." It was a pointless remark, for the fact was only too obvious.

Feverishly Jennings sought some fire-fighting weapon; and as the nearest thing to hand was the parcel of fish he grabbed it from the table and dropped it on the flames billowing up from the floor. There was a dull thud, a spurt of smoke and the fire was out.

"Whew! Talk about a ghastly bish!" Jennings wiped imaginary beads of perspiration from his brow.

"What happened?"

"The developing dish was a celluloid one – that's what! I ought to have used an enamel one, really."

"I should think you jolly well ought!" returned Darbishire indignantly. "You are a dangerous maniac, Jen. Every one knows celluloid burns like blinko."

"Don't get in a flap. It's all over now."

But it wasn't all over. Acrid fumes of burnt plastic were spreading over the room like a dense fog. Jennings coughed; politely at first, but as the fumes thickened he was unable to control the tickle in his nose and throat. Then the gaseous fog reached Darbishire by the window and paroxysms of coughing echoed round the darkened room.

"Open the window, quick," gasped Jennings.

Darbishire fumbled with the catch, threw up the lower sash and poked his head out into the cool morning air. "Phew, that's

37

better! You've no idea how decent fresh air smells when you've just had a shortage of it."

He removed his spectacles and dabbed his streaming eyes. Then he replaced his glasses and looked through them, and what he saw caused him to shoot back into the dark room and slam the window shut.

"What's up?" Jennings' voice came out of the darkness.

"Mr Wilkins! He's outside on the quad. He saw my head pop out."

"Oh, golly!"

"Yes, and that's not all! He saw it pop back again, too, and he must have wondered…"

"Ssh!"

Both boys stood still and listened; the room was not yet clear of fumes and it was all they could do to stifle their coughs.

They had not long to wait. Footsteps sounded on the gravel outside and a purposeful knuckle tapped on the glass.

"Open this window at once!" Mr Wilkins' tone indicated that he meant to investigate the mystery of the popping head without delay. But he could not see through a coat of black paint and the inhabitants of the dark room were overcome by a sudden deafness.

Mr Wilkins rapped again. No answer. What on earth could those silly little boys be playing at, he wondered? Had they hurried out of the room at his approach? He decided to find out.

The footsteps scrunched again and died away as he turned the corner of the building and entered the front door.

"Oh, golly, he's coming round," moaned Darbishire. "Whatever shall we do? He knows we weren't developing because of having the window open."

"We'd better open it again, now he's gone and let another basinful of this smoke out." Jennings suggested. "He'll be bashing on the door in half a sec and we'll have to let him in. Buck up, we've no time to hang about!"

With one accord they threw themselves into a frenzied scurry of tidying-up. Darbishire flung wide the window, and then took off his jacket and fanned the air. Jennings gathered up the charred remains of the developing dish and dropped them in the sink. The roll of negative and a bottle of hypo were displayed on the table to show how busily they were absorbed in photography, and in a few moments the dark room had almost assumed its normal appearance.

Only one thing seemed oddly out of place: behind the door was a medium-sized parcel of plaice, mackerel and cod.

4

Conjuring Trick

L P Wilkins, Esq., MA (Cantab.), was a man of vigorous action. He made no secret of his out-flanking movement, but strode heavily along the corridor and rattled the handle of the dark room door.

"Open this door, immediately!"

Mr Wilkins had a voice which would have been audible above the clatter and roar of a brass foundry. It was useless, then, to plead inattention or hardness of hearing. What was to be done? Darbishire stood on one leg and gaped in dismay at the parcel behind the door.

"Oh, golly, we shouldn't have done this! He'll see it when he comes in, and there's just nowhere to hide the beastly stuff. My father says that... Gosh, Jen, what*ever* are you doing?"

Jennings was doing the only thing he *could* do. He was tucking the parcel of fish under the tail of his jacket; then he took up an unnatural stance with his hands clasped firmly behind his back.

"How many more times have I got to tell you to open the door?" Mr Wilkins was growing impatient, and the panels quivered and heaved as though a small bulldozer were at work on a demolition site.

Darbishire hastily drew back the bolt and the door flew open.

"Now what on earth's going on in here?" But Mr Wilkins' nose answered this question for him as he inhaled the atmosphere. "I – I – Corwumph! Something's been burning!"

"Yes, sir. A developing dish caught fire by accident, but it's all right now, sir," Jennings assured him.

"We'll soon see about that." Mr Wilkins strode across the threshold and stood sniffing like a bloodhound. He was determined to be thorough: he examined the charred remains in the sink, knocked the roll of negative off the table and upset the hypo bottle in his efforts to leave no stone unturned. As he moved about the room, Jennings moved too and took care never to turn his back.

Finally the master spoke: "I don't know much about photography, but if it's necessary to set the place on fire and befoul the atmosphere for miles around, it's not the hobby I took it for. Have you boys got leave to be in here?"

"Well, sir, last night Mr Hind said I could develop my film, but I don't actually think he knows we're in here at the moment, if you see what I mean," Jennings replied.

"So you're here without permission?"

"Well, in a manner of speaking, I suppose we are, sir."

"Never mind the manner of speaking, Jennings, or I shall do some speaking in a manner you won't appreciate. And what's more, you're up before the rising bell again! Go up to my room and wait for me."

"Yes, Sir."

Jennings backed out of the doorway like a medieval courtier in the presence of royalty. The clasped hands and the forwards thrust of the shoulders gave him an air of studious detachment which he was far from feeling: but he could not relax his attitude without dropping the parcel.

Darbishire did his best to cover his friend's retreat and as they went along the corridor he whispered: "What are we going to do? We can't take it up to Old Wilkie's room."

He bitterly regretted, now, that he had ever taken a hand in the venture. Everything had gone wrong. And if, in addition to their other troubles, the fish was to be discovered after Mr Carter's instructions of the previous day, it would shed a new and sinister light upon their early morning activities.

"If only we could dump the beastly stuff somewhere!" Jennings said as they climbed the stairs. But it would have been asking for trouble to stray from their route, with Mr Wilkins so hard upon their heels. For a moment Jennings considered slipping the parcel inside an empty laundry basket on the first landing, but Matron made an untimely appearance just as he was about to lift the lid, and the attempt had to be abandoned.

Along the landing and up the next flight of stairs they dragged their unwilling footsteps, while their hopes of finding a hiding-place faded with every yard. At last they reached Mr Wilkins' door.

"Surely there's *somewhere*," groaned Darbishire, looking despairingly along the top landing. "He'll be here in a second; he's talking to Matron just below."

Jennings wasted no time. "Open his door quick!" he ordered.

Darbishire stared aghast. "Have you gone stark raving bats! We can't hide it in there!"

"There's nowhere else, is there? Anyway it's only for now. We'll get it back afterwards."

With some misgiving Darbishire pushed open the master's door and the boys scuttled inside; but luck was against them. Mr Wilkins' study was furnished with a table, three chairs, a locked cupboard and a glass-fronted bookcase. There wasn't enough cover to hide a shrimp, let alone a medium-sized parcel of fish. And heavy footsteps were sounding on the stairs.

"Nip out on the landing and keep him talking," urged Jennings.

"What about?"

"Anything you like. Just chat naturally."

"I can never think of anything to say when I'm trying to be natural," Darbishire objected, "and it seems crazy to start talking about the weather…"

"Oh, go *on*, Darbi. Do as I tell you!"

Unwillingly, Darbishire left his friend and hurried through the door. The master was at the top of the stairs now and his expression suggested that he was in no mood to be delayed with polite remarks about the weather.

"What were you doing in my room, Darbishire?" he demanded.

"Er – just coming out, sir."

"I can see that, you silly little boy. I distinctly told you to wait outside my room, not to go blundering in. You and Jennings cause enough chaos when you get loose in a dark room; heaven knows what you'd get up to in a civilised sitting-room. Blow the place up, I expect!"

In two strides Mr Wilkins was through the door and inside his study. Darbishire followed, feeling empty inside and trying to keep his mind off what was going to happen next. It could be only a matter of seconds before… Darbishire blinked through his spectacles and then opened his eyes in astonishment.

Jennings was standing on the hearthrug; his hands hung freely at his sides and there was no bulge beneath his jacket. Darbishire cast quick, anxious glances about the room; the furniture was exactly as it had been when he had left ten seconds before.

Then where on earth – and Darbishire searched his mind in vain for an answer to the riddle – where on earth had Jennings hidden the parcel?

From his earliest years Darbishire had always been fascinated by conjuring tricks. At Christmas parties he would watch spellbound as some talented friend of the family produced a string of knotted handkerchiefs from a top hat or caused the ace of spades to vanish into thin air and come to light in a flower pot. But never had he seen a trick to equal the *Mystery of the Disappearing Fish-bag!*

The thing just wasn't possible! Less than a minute before, Jennings had been wandering distractedly round the room clutching the parcel beneath his jacket. Now, by some uncanny sleight of hand, the unwanted bulge had dissolved into the atmosphere.

Darbishire peered round the room seeking the solution to this paragon of parlour tricks. Was there an unsuspected trapdoor beneath the carpet? Had the bookcase a false bottom or a sliding panel? Perhaps the trick was done by mass-hypnotism or the use of mirrors. Perhaps, even…

"What on earth is the matter with you, Darbishire? Have you lost something?" Mr Wilkins' voice cut into the boy's speculations and brought him back to reality with a start.

"Er – no, sir. Or rather, yes, thank you, sir, but it doesn't matter really."

"Then stop gaping at the furniture like a village idiot, and listen to me. It's quite obvious that neither of you are fit to develop your own photographs – quite apart from the fact that you were doing so without permission and before the rising bell."

Mr Wilkins was justifiably annoyed. Every morning before breakfast he liked to take a brisk walk, swinging his arms vigorously and inhaling deep lungfuls of fresh air. This morning, however, he had been obliged to cut short his health-giving exercise and grope about a dingy dark room, breathing the pungent fumes of what he wrongly imagined to be photographic chemicals.

"I've just about had enough of this stupid nonsense," he continued. "You will both do an hour's work for me on Saturday afternoon and take a black stripe for your conduct books. And I warn you that if there's any more of this – this juvenile delinquency – I'll... Well, you'd better look out!"

"Yes, sir."

Outside on the landing, Jennings heaved a sigh of relief and said: "Well, that wasn't so bad, was it? Or rather, it'd have been a wizard sight worse if he'd known what had *really* been cooking in the dark room, because..."

"Yes, but where is it?" Darbishire broke in urgently.

"The dark room? You know that as well as I do. Downstairs through the basement."

Darbishire danced with impatience. "No, you prehistoric clodpoll! Where's the parcel of fish?"

"Oh, that! Well, as a matter of fact I had a rare brainstroke after you'd beetled out. You see, I knew I'd got to do something, quick."

"And what did you do, quick?"

"I bunged the whole caboodle up Old Wilkie's chimney."

"What!... Oh, gosh!" Darbishire stared at his friend in wide-eyed dismay. Of all the places to put it.

"What else could I do?" Jennings defended himself. "It's all very fine for you to stand there 'Oh, goshing,' but I bet you couldn't have thought of anything better on the spur of the moment."

45

Now that the *Mystery of the Disappearing Fish-bag* was solved, Darbishire began to think that perhaps it wasn't such a good trick after all.

"But we can't leave it there for ever and ever," he protested. "Mr Wilkins would have to wear a respirator and summon the insanitary spectre."

"Summon the *what?*" Into Jennings' mind floated the picture of an unhygienic ghost haunting the master's study.

"I mean the sanitary inspector," Darbishire corrected himself. He was still feeling rather confused.

"Don't get in a flap, Darbi; I'll think of something. It's goodbye to our early breakfast, though; by the time we get it back, it'll be hardly worth eating."

As though to compensate them for their loss, the breakfast bell rang at that moment, and Jennings and Darbishire joined the stream of boys which flowed from the dormitories and cascaded down the stairs like a human waterfall.

"Where have you two been?" Venables demanded from across the table, as they sat down to breakfast. "Atkinson and I have been searching the dorm for you. We wanted to demonstrate our famous patent invention of putting our pullovers on before taking our pyjama jackets off."

"Why?" inquired Darbishire without enthusiasm. He felt he had seen enough tricks for one morning.

"Well, why not? It's a good idea," said Atkinson. "We get dressed first and then work our pyjama-tops down our shirt sleeves and out at the wrist. Pity you missed it."

Jennings hastened to explain their absence. "Mr Hind said I could do my film in the dark room last night, and just because a developing dish went swoosh when we were using it as a frying-pan, Old Wilkie came charging in like an armoured column and kicked up a hoo-hah."

"What did you want to fry it for?" demanded Venables. It seemed an odd thing to do with a roll of film.

"Oh, I don't mean the photos; we were frying the fish."

"What fish?"

"The ones in Mr Wilkins' chimney."

This was too difficult for Venables, and it was some time before he had sorted the jumbled explanation into some semblance of order. Then he said: "Well, you've got nothing to worry about. It should be pretty easy to nip in and hoik it down when Mr Wilkins isn't there. I bet I could do it without being copped."

"All very well for you to talk! I'd like to see what sort of a bish you'd make of it," said Jennings.

It was, of course, the only solution and he had already made up his mind to try it when conditions were favourable. All the same, he was not going to let Venables or anyone else suggest that the task would be easy.

Darbishire made a poor breakfast that morning. As he toyed with his baked beans – a poor substitute for fried fish, he thought – the question of retrieving the parcel was uppermost in his mind. Jennings had bungled things badly; perhaps the keen brain of C E J Darbishire could save the situation. He would go to Mr Wilkins' room and knock boldly on the door; if there was no answer, it would mean the coast was clear. If there *was* an answer – well, that would have to be faced when the time came. In any case the sooner this miserable business was cleared up the better, for today was Monday, and that evening he and Jennings hoped to start printing the first number of the *Form Three Times*.

Mr Wilkins was enjoying his after-breakfast pipe when the first knock sounded on his door. He called: "Come in!" and was surprised to hear a pattering scurry outside, as though some heavy-footed rabbit were making for cover on tiptoe. He hurled open the door and caught sight of a curly-headed figure disappearing down the corridor.

"Darbishire!" he shouted.

The figure skidded to a stop, and bent down to retrieve a house shoe which had been travelling too fast to obey the halt summons.

"Sir?"

"What on earth are you doing?"

"Putting my shoe on, sir."

"I can see that, you silly little boy. That doesn't explain why you knocked at my door and then skated off down the corridor. Do you want to see me?"

"No, sir. Not specially, thank you, sir."

"Then what *do* you want?"

Darbishire considered. What he had *really* wanted was to find the room empty, but that was not the sort of answer that would be well received; and as the owner of a tender conscience he could not bring himself to say anything which was not strictly true. What else did he want? There must be *something* if only he could think what it was. At last he said: "Well, sir, I *could* do with a stamp, sir; then I could write to my grandmother."

"Then why not ask for one in a civilised manner?" simmered Mr Wilkins. He led the way into his study and took down the folder in which he kept stamps for the boys' letters.

Darbishire stood in the doorway and cast furtive glances at the fireplace. It looked all right, but... Was it his imagination, or was there a faint tang in the air? He sniffed, and was still not sure; so he inhaled a series of long, deep breaths – and was suddenly aware that Mr Wilkins was looking at him in a puzzled manner.

"What are you snuffling for? Playing at bloodhounds?" the master inquired.

Darbishire's lungs were so full of air that he could not reply without risking a minor explosion. Instead he held his breath, hoping that Mr Wilkins would turn his attention to other matters. He hoped in vain, and five seconds ticked by while the master grew more bewildered and Darbishire became pinker and pinker in the face. Then, with a sound like a punctured bicycle tyre, he gave up the unequal struggle.

"I was just holding my breath, sir," he explained, somewhat unnecessarily.

"Well, don't do it here," said Mr Wilkins. "My study's not the place for breath-holding contests or any other sort of nonsensical buffoonery. Here, take your stamp and go and pretend you're a vacuum brake somewhere where I can't hear you."

"Yes, sir."

Darbishire was a frequent visitor to Mr Wilkins' study that day; but on every occasion he found the room occupied and had to improvise some reason for his visit. At break, he bought another stamp. Just before lunch he called to ask Mr Wilkins for his autograph. After lunch, he looked in to ask whether "Sir" could tell him what the time was.

By five o'clock, Mr Wilkins was tiring of his visitor: he had sold him four stamps, lent him an india-rubber, undone an almost inextricable knot in the laces of his football boots and admired a snapshot of the Rev. and Mrs Darbishire on the beach at Bournemouth. It seemed that the only way to secure a few minutes' peace would be to go for a walk. So Mr Wilkins went.

"If that problem child comes knocking at my door again, he's going to be unlucky," he said to himself, as he strode down the drive swinging his arms vigorously.

As it happened, Darbishire *was* unlucky, for he missed his chance while the coast was clear. He, also, had grown tired of his visits to the study, and could think of no further excuses to offer. So he denied himself the doubtful pleasure of a ninth trip and went to look for Jennings instead.

He found him in the tuck-box room, gathering together the news items for the first edition of the *Form Three Times*.

"Where have you been, Darbi?" his friend demanded. "Every break today you've beetled off somewhere just when I wanted you to help me with the photos for our magazine."

"I've been doing a special priority secret service job, getting that bag back," Darbishire explained.

"Goodo! What have you done with it?"

"Well, I haven't exactly quite got it, yet. But I've kept Old Wilkie under pretty close observation all day, and, honestly, Jen, I don't know how we're ever going to get in there. He sticks in that room like a hermit in his cell."

"He won't feel like staying there much longer, if we don't get that parcel out. Another few days and he'll begin to wonder what's gone wrong with the ventilation."

"Oh, golly, I wish we'd never done it!" lamented Darbishire. "We must just keep very calm and think out what to do. My father knows a quotation from *Horace* about keeping a balanced mind in adversity."

Jennings snorted. "It'd be more to the point if *Horace* had told him one about how to get things out of chimneys. I can't think why you have to clutter the place up with your father's famous wise sayings; we've got enough troubles on our plates already."

Darbishire sank wearily onto a tuck-box and said nothing. It was at times like this that what his father said seemed truer than ever.

5

The "Form Three Times"

There seemed little point in visiting Mr Wilkins' room again that evening, and Jennings decided that an expedition would have more chance of success if the attempt was postponed until later in the week.

So during tea that evening he thought out a workable plan: Wednesday was a half-holiday, when Mr Wilkins would be in charge of their football game. As soon as the final whistle sounded, Jennings could hurry indoors and retrieve the evidence, while Darbishire delayed the referee on the football pitch with abstruse questions about the off-side rule.

It was a simple scheme which gave every promise of running smoothly; even the short delay in its execution would not matter because there was little risk of the well-wrapped parcel proclaiming its presence in a cool chimney before Wednesday. The planners charged their beakers and drank to the success of their scheme in weak tea, for now they could devote the evening to the important task of printing the *Form Three Times*.

There was a clear hour before bedtime when the editors settled down in the hobbies room, armed with their notebooks, the *Ideal* printing outfit and the photographs of the *Sainte Marie*.

The remaining photographs on the film were not altogether successful, for Jennings' failure to wind the spool between each snapshot had produced some odd results. A picture of Darbishire posing by the garden roller was disfigured by the ghostly apparition of Bromwich floating in mid-air in the background; while a more freakish double exposure, taken from the football pitch, gave the impression that the goalkeeper was trying to save Mr Wilkins' head from going through the library window.

Regretfully, the editors dropped the useless prints into the waste-paper basket and started to set up the headlines for the front page. For a while they worked happily, fitting the little pellets into the wooden slots with infinite patience, and producing a line of print which, though unevenly spaced, was certainly legible.

But when three-quarters of an hour had ticked away and the first paragraph was still unfinished, they began to realise that their enthusiasm had blinded them to a serious drawback: the *Ideal Junior Printing Outfit* was all very well for dashing off brief notes of thanks, but a full-sized magazine was a different matter altogether. Some words were taking more than a minute to piece together, and every now and then progress came to a standstill as the printers searched feverishly through their stock for some letter which had strayed from its place in the queue of alphabetical order.

"This is hopeless! We'll never get finished at this rate," complained the chief editor; his patience had been wearing thin ever since his assistant had dropped a question mark into the inkwell. "There's twelve pages to do yet, and we're still up at the top of page one. It'll take us about…" There was a pause while he sought the answer in mental arithmetic… "It'll take about ninety-six weeks if we don't step up our output a bit, and all the news will be as stale as buns, years before it gets printed."

The assistant editor rose from examining the cracks between the floorboards where he had been carrying on a search for straying letters. "I don't want to say anything against your Aunt Angela's generous present," he remarked, "but if she'd only given you a proper typewriter, we might be getting somewhere – if only we knew how to type."

"Gosh, yes, that's not a bad idea! Let's type it," Jennings replied. "We can still use the printing outfit for headlines and stop-press and stuff like that."

"That's all very well, but we haven't got a typewriter."

"No, but Mr Carter has," said Jennings promptly. "And he's always on at us to get cracking on highbrow stuff like magazines and wall-papers."

"The *Form Three Times* isn't wall-paper. It's a wall newspaper, and that's quite different. Besides, would Mr Carter let us borrow the machine?"

"I'm pretty sure he wouldn't. But if we ask and he says No, he may feel a bit uncomfortable, after all he's said, and offer to type it for us."

Mr Carter was marking essays in his study when the polite rap on the door announced that he was about to receive visitors. He guessed from the sound of the knock that they had come to ask a favour; for it was neither the timid tap of one who reports for punishment, nor the urgent panel-beating of the bearer of important news.

"Well, Jennings, what can I do for you?" the master asked as the two boys ranged themselves before the writing table.

"Well, sir, Darbishire and me hoped you'd do us a favour, sir."

Mr Carter winced. He had a tidy, grammatical mind. "No; Darbishire and *I* hoped you would do us a favour, Jennings," he corrected.

Jennings looked surprised. "Did you, sir? Darbishire never told me."

"I mean, Jennings, that you should say Darbishire and I, not Darbishire and *me*."

"I see, sir. Well, would you do Darbishire and I a favour please sir?"

Mr Carter closed his eyes. Very patiently he said: "This time, Jennings, it's correct to say Darbishire and *me*."

Jennings felt that the object of their visit was being obscured by grammatical argument. "Well, anyway, sir, the point is that Darbishire and I or me, are writing a magazine and we wondered if we could borrow your typewriter to biff out parts of it on, sir."

"I'm afraid not. It's not a toy, you know."

"I know, sir. That's what we thought you'd say. I hope you didn't mind our asking, sir." He made no move to go, but stood silent and hopeful.

Mr Carter guessed what the silent hope was about and said: "Of course there's just a slight chance that I might be willing to type it for you. Let me see first if it's worth doing."

He glanced through the items in the notebooks. From time to time he groaned at the literary style and tut-tutted over the handwriting; but then, those were matters which could be remedied when the magazine appeared in its finished form. Finally he laid down the notebooks and said: "Very well: I'll type it for you. Is this all there is?"

"There's just a bit more, but we can do that on our printing outfit, sir," Jennings answered. "We thought of putting in a couple of competitions to help fill up space a bit, but we haven't decided what they're to be yet."

Mr Carter narrowed his eyes as he glanced once more at the pencilled scrawl before him. "Why not have a handwriting competition?" he suggested. "Anything that would improve the writing in this school would be worth trying."

"Good idea, sir. That'll do wizardly for one," Darbishire agreed. "And for the second one we could have…what?"

Again Mr Carter sought inspiration from the rough copy in his hands. "What this magazine needs is a higher literary standard. I think you might persuade your readers to try their hand at writing an original poem or something of that sort."

"Rather, sir. Super idea!" said Jennings. "And we could offer really decent valuable prizes such as – er, well, double-decker sponge cakes, for instance."

"But we haven't *got* any super double-decker sponge cakes," the assistant editor pointed out.

"No, I know, but *if* we had! Think what decent prizes they'd make! Why, anyone with any sense would have a bash at writing a chunk of poetry if there was a sponge cake going for a prize." Jennings' eyes shone with enthusiasm as he warmed to his theme. "And what's more, I'm pretty sure my Aunt Angela would send me a couple if I told her they were to encourage poetry and stuff. She's ever so keen on culture."

The first number of the *Form Three Times* appeared on the noticeboard the following morning, and created a considerable stir throughout the school. Here and there an item of news was printed in the vivid mauve hue of the *Ideal Junior Printing Outfit*, but the main part of the journal was neatly typed, and – thanks to Mr Carter – correctly spelled.

Atkinson was thrilled with the account of his year-old discovery of the caterpillar in the cabbage, and stood for minutes at a time, staring at his name in typed capitals. Binns was secretly disappointed that the riddle of the missing football boot had not been included. He had found his boot by this time, but he would have been more than willing to hide it again in order to make his story sound more probable.

By break-time, everyone had heard about the magazine: everyone except Bromwich, who was a lone wolf and a law unto himself. Jennings came across him in the tuck-box room, working on an air-conditioning plant for his rabbit hutch.

"I say, Bromo, have you seen my magazine?" Jennings began excitedly.

"No, I haven't," answered Bromwich curtly. "You're always losing things and expecting everyone to know where they are."

"No, you clodpoll, I haven't lost it! I mean have you seen it up on the wall?"

Bromwich looked interested. "Golly! However did it get up there?" he wanted to know. Patiently Jennings explained, and Bromwich decided to go and see for himself.

When they arrived in the common room they had difficulty in getting near the noticeboard for the throng of readers who were absorbing once again the news which they had known about for some time. However, the front page photograph of the crew of the *Sainte Marie* was new to them all and caused a certain amount of speculation. Jennings had forgotten to write a caption for it and opinions differed as to whether they were Chinese bandits or miners queuing up for pit-head baths.

But it was the two competitions which attracted the greatest interest. After all, here were double-decker sponge cakes being freely offered, and what more could anyone want than that?

"I could do with one of those sponge cakes," said Bromwich.

"So could I. I've a jolly good mind to have a shot at writing a home-made poem," said Atkinson thoughtfully. He turned to Venables, who stood beside him in the queue. "You ought to walk away with the other comp, Venables. Your writing's super!"

"Oh, I don't know," replied Venables modestly. "I haven't decided which one to go in for yet." He edged his way forward to the board and read out the rules which Darbishire had hastily added in pencil after the magazine had been typed.

"*All competition entries must be in by Friday week. Do not write on one side of the paper...?*" He broke off puzzled, and then shouted: "Hey, Darbishire, come over here. Your rules are stark raving crackers! If we can't write on one side of the paper, what *can* we do?"

The assistant editor was standing, proud and important, on the fringe of the group. "You can write on the other side, can't you?" he asked reasonably.

"How are we to know which the other side is?"

"It doesn't really matter. It's just that it's easier for the editors to correct if you only write on one side at a time; or rather..."

"You mean, we mustn't write on more than both sides altogether?" asked Atkinson.

"Yes – er, no, you coot. It's obvious what it means if you've got any sense."

Venables turned again to the rules. "*Take your made-up poem or about twenty lines of your best handwriting to the Competition Editor's Office, Tuck-Box Room, and don't forget to write 'Comp' in the top left-hand corner.*"

"I can't reach the top left-hand corner of the tuck-box room unless I stand on the table," Atkinson objected.

"It doesn't mean that, you ancient ruin! You're just not *trying* to understand." Darbishire clutched his forehead in exasperation, and the action knocked his glasses askew so that they sat across his nose at the angle of a percentage sign. He had spent some time in compiling the rules and had gone to the trouble of adding: *The Editor's indecision is final.* It was, therefore, understandable that he resented these flippant remarks.

"Come on, Venables; Darbi's getting batey," said Atkinson. "Let's go and have a shot at making up a few wads of poetry."

When Jennings awoke next morning the thought of food was uppermost in his mind. There was nothing unusual about this, for it was one of his favourite waking thoughts; but on this occasion it brought no feeling of joy. Fish and sponge cakes: both were items on the day's programme which called for skilful handling.

He knew he could rely on Darbishire to help him in the first project, but the second depended upon the co-operation of his Aunt Angela and this was a cause for anxiety. His aunt was kindhearted, but she had an uncertain, sieve-like memory; vague promises to make sponge cakes would be of no use if the goods failed to arrive in time for the prize-giving. Already the more legible writers had begun uncrossing their nibs and searching for clean blotting paper, while the poets were scratching their heads and looking thoughtful.

Aunt Angela's help must be enlisted without delay, Jennings decided. He would write to her at once and underline his requirements twice in red ink: *two double-decker jam sponge cakes, not less than approx. nine inches across, please.* That should do the trick!

He started the letter during morning break and finished it in Mr Hind's history lesson. The next problem was the clearance of Mr Wilkins' chimney, and the two boys put the finishing touches to their plan as they changed for football that afternoon.

"Now, don't forget, Darbi, we've got to get cracking on this wheeze just as though it was an important military operation," Jennings explained. "I shall be the commandos doing the dangerous part, while you're the supporting troops engaging the enemy to give me cover. Zero hour's directly after football, and we beetle off to action stations as soon as Old Wilkie blows for time."

"Hadn't we better synchronise our watches?" inquired the supporting troops.

"How can we? We shan't be wearing them during the game. It's all quite simple, really. You just have to keep him nattering on the pitch till you see me wave from the quad. That means I've liberated the parcel and dumped it out of sight somewhere."

The scheme, though flawless in theory, did not work out so smoothly as they had hoped.

The weather was blustery that afternoon; the game was scrappy and Mr Wilkins was not sorry when the time came for him to blow the final whistle. As the echoes of the shrill blast died away, Darbishire approached the referee with a look of earnest inquiry on his features.

"Sir, please sir, would you explain something, please sir?"

"Well, what is it? Hurry up, I don't want to hang about here all day."

"Well, sir, if, say, supposing I was centre forward for the white shirts and I kicked the ball to Temple, who was on the right wing with nobody in front of him, and he missed it and, say, Binns, who was left half for the colours, got it and headed it to Martin-Jones, only it was intercepted by Atkinson, who was a white, and he hoofed it down to Bromwich at left back, and Thompson was coming up behind him in a coloured shirt with no one in front of him – would it be off-side, sir?"

Mr Wilkins was out of his depth. "Would *who* be off-side?"

"Well, say Thompson, for instance, sir. Or if not him, then one of the others – if say supposing, just before that, somebody else, like Brown or Paterson or someone had beetled up from nowhere into the other side's penalty area, sir?"

Mr Wilkins was unwilling to give a decision on such tangled data. "It depends on who played the ball last, and anyway, I can't follow what you're talking about. Come up to my room with me and I'll lend you a copy of the laws of the game; then you can work it out for yourself." He turned and made for the touchline.

Darbishire hopped from one foot to the other in frustration and grief. Jennings would not have had nearly enough time to carry out his part of the programme. "Oh, sir, wait! Don't go, sir, yet, sir, please sir! Do you think I played well, this afternoon, sir?"

"Frankly, no."

"Oh, well, if I go in goal now, will you give me a few practice shots to save, sir?"

"Not in these shoes, thank you. Besides, it's too cold to stay outside. I'm going indoors to put a match to my fire. I'm expecting the Headmaster at four o'clock and he won't want to…"

Mr Wilkins broke off and looked more closely at the small figure hopping round him in agitated circles. There was something unusual about the boy's appearance, and for a moment he couldn't think what it was. Then he said: "Where are your spectacles, Darbishire?"

"My spectacles!" Darbishire bit his lip and his hand rose to his face in alarm. "Oh, goodness, sir! I must have lost them on the pitch. I know I had them when the game started."

Mr Wilkins tut-tutted at the everlasting carelessness of small boys. Then he improvised a search party of everyone who had not already disappeared indoors, and for ten minutes they picked their way gingerly up and down the field. It was Temple who found the missing glasses hanging perilously from the goal net by one earpiece.

"Coo, thanks ever so much, Temple. I was getting worried about them," beamed Darbishire. He remembered now; he had hung them on the net for safety when he had been sent to keep goal during the second half: oddly enough, it made little difference to his performance as a goalkeeper whether he could see the ball clearly or not.

Darbishire replaced his glasses and thanked the unwilling searchers a dozen times. As he followed them off the field he couldn't help thinking how strange it was that his carefully planned delaying tactics had failed, yet his object had been achieved by genuine means. It was safe now for Mr Wilkins to go indoors, and light fifty fires if he wanted to. Jennings would have had plenty of time.

But Jennings was finding things more difficult than he had bargained for. He had hurried off the field at the scheduled time and reached Mr Wilkins' room safely. No one was about, so he opened the door and went in. A fire was laid in the grate, but fortunately it had not been lighted. That was a bit of luck, he decided. If anyone had put a match to it while the chimney was still blocked it would have… But nobody had, so why waste time thinking about it!

In two strides he was at the fireplace; then, kneeling he reached up the chimney – and his clutching fingers closed on empty air!

For a moment panic seized him. Mr Wilkins must have found it! Then reason returned and told him that this was not possible. Mr Wilkins was not the sort of person to keep such a discovery secret. There would have been an immediate outcry, with alarms and excursions to all parts of the building in an effort to find the culprit.

Jennings groped again and poked his head into the fireplace, but he could see nothing. He must have pushed it farther up than he had thought; perhaps the chimney had a ledge; perhaps it had…

Jennings froze! Footsteps were approaching along the corridor – heavy, adult-sounding footsteps. Would they pass by or would they come in?

He was not kept long in suspense, for it was barely three seconds later that the door swung open and M W B Pemberton-Oakes, Esq., Headmaster, stood on the threshold.

6

The Incomplete Anglers

Acutely embarrassed, Jennings scrambled to his feet while the Headmaster stood silently noting the grimy hands and the freckles of soot.

"May I inquire what you're doing, Jennings?"

It was impossible to tell from the Headmaster's tone whether he was surprised or angry, for he was a man who seldom betrayed his feelings.

"I was – er, I was just putting my head up the chimney, sir."

"So I observe; and I am somewhat at a loss to understand why."

Jennings shifted his feet uncomfortably. "I just wanted to see if I could see up, sir."

"I see." Mr Pemberton-Oakes had been dealing with inquiring minds for so long that the explanation seemed reasonable. Thirty-five years of schoolmastering had taught him that eleven-year-old boys would perform the most extraordinary actions for reasons which no adult could hope to understand. They would stand on their heads without apparent cause and paint walrus moustaches on their faces with water-colours; they would smear their fingers with marmalade and plasticene and then set about some task requiring delicacy of touch – such as dealing a pack of cards

or practising the violin. Thus it came as no surprise to Mr
Pemberton-Oakes to hear that Jennings should feel an urge to
poke his head up the chimney to see how much blackness met
his gaze. Such actions were only to be expected. His eye
travelled down from the soot-streaked face to the muddy
boots.

"I assume, Jennings, that Mr Wilkins has sent you here to
await his arrival," said the Headmaster. "But that is no reason
why you should have come upstairs in your football boots. Go
down and change them at once."

"Yes, sir."

As Jennings left the room he noticed that Mr Pemberton-
Oakes made no movement to follow. Obviously he had come
to see Mr Wilkins and intended to wait in the study until the
master arrived. What on earth was to be done?

Jennings descended to the boot-lockers in a daze of
indecision and he was still staring at his football boots with
unseeing eyes when Darbishire slapped him between the
shoulder blades a few minutes later.

"All fixed up nicely?" Darbishire inquired brightly. "I kept
Old Wilkie out of the way, but you never came and gave me
the all-clear. Just as well you snaffled that parcel when you did,
because he's just gone upstairs to light his fire."

"What!" Jennings spun round like a weather-cock.

"Yes; he's making it cosy because the Archbeako's coming to
see him." And then something in his friend's glassy expression
spread a horrible doubt through his mind. "You – you don't
mean you've made a bish of it?"

Jennings nodded. "The Archbeako ankled in in the middle
and ticked me off for sticking my head up the chimney with
my football boots on."

"Oh, fish-hooks! Why didn't you take your boots off first?"

"I wouldn't have been able to see any better if I had – I haven't got luminous toe-nails."

"No, what I meant was…oh, never mind!" Darbishire sounded badly rattled. "The damage is done now, and there'll be the most frantic hoo-hah when it all comes out."

"When *what* comes out? The news or the parcel?"

"Both, I suppose. Firstly we didn't get rid of the beastly stuff when Mr Carter told us to; second, we opened up a fried fish shop in the dark room; third, Mr Wilkins will get asphyxiated when he lights his fire, and fourth – well, anything might happen. My father says that when sorrows come, they…"

But Jennings was not listening. He was frowning into space and racking his brains for a way to meet this new crisis. Suddenly, he smote his brow and said: "I've got it, Darbi! We'll go fishing."

Darbishire stared at his friend in horror-struck amazement. "We wizard well *won't!*" he said decisively. "I've had enough of that sort of caper to last me for a long time. Anyone arranging fishing trips, or even serving it up with chips, can include me out of the party, thanks very much."

"No, listen; we can't get at it from below, so we'll have a bash from above. All we need is a hook and a long piece of string, and there we are."

The essence of Jennings' plan lay in the fact that Mr Wilkins' chimney emerged onto a flat roof, surrounded by a stone balustrade. Very properly, the roof was out of bounds, but it could be reached from an attic window which opened directly onto it. If the parcel was not too tightly wedged, might it not be possible to retrieve it by lowering a hook down the chimney?

"H'm! It *might!* And it might *not!*" objected Darbishire, when the details of the scheme became clear.

"It's our only chance," Jennings urged. "Let's get changed quickly; then I'll go and bag a hook from somewhere while you scavenge for a bit of string."

They changed out of their football clothes in record time and as he was bundling his sweater on to his peg, Jennings' eye lighted upon a small brass hook screwed into the wall beside it. Its real purpose was to accommodate the overflow of football garments, but it would serve equally well for a roof-angling expedition. He was unscrewing it when Darbishire returned from a scavenge hunt round the boot-lockers, clutching a tangled mass of knotted string.

"How long would you say Wilkie's chimney is?" the scavenger asked.

Jennings considered. "About as long as a fairly medium sized piece of string, I should think."

"Yes, that's what I thought. This ought to do the trick, if I can get the knots out; and I'll join my football boot lace on the end just to be on the safe side."

After that they found a broken door-knob in the waste-paper basket and tied it on as a weight, to ensure that the hook would go right down the chimney.

Then, armed with hook, line and sinker, they tip-toed up to the attic, climbed out onto the roof and hurried towards their action station.

For the second time in twenty minutes zero hour had arrived!

Mr Wilkins sat on a hard, upright chair beside his unlighted fire and hoped that the Headmaster would not stay too long. It was not that Mr Wilkins was unsociable, but rather that his visitor was occupying the only comfortable chair in the room, and he had been looking forward to sitting there himself.

However, Mr Pemberton-Oakes seemed in no hurry to cut short the discussion on the mathematics syllabus which was the reason for his visit. Already he had expounded his views for over quarter of an hour, while his assistant said: "Yes, I quite agree," at regular intervals.

"Now this question of a weekly algebra test for all forms," the Headmaster was saying. "I consider it a matter of the greatest importance that boys should be made to check their answers in order to avoid absurd and incongruous results."

"Yes, sir, I quite agree," said Mr Wilkins.

"Furthermore, we must impress upon them the practical value of algebraical problems by showing them that x's and y's are merely symbols representing…"

But this time, Mr Wilkins wasn't listening. He had just caught sight of something even more absurd and incongruous than an unchecked algebra result, and he was staring at the fireplace, his eyes bulging with bewilderment. Surely, he must be mistaken! It must be some trick of the fading light. He sat bolt upright and blinked; but when he looked again at the fireplace, the *thing* was still there.

"…because, unless we succeed in stimulating the boys' interest and holding their attention, all our work will be so much…"

The Headmaster stopped, suddenly aware that his assistant's interest was no longer being stimulated, nor his interest held by the question of the weekly algebra test. "Really, Wilkins, considering how important the matter is, I think you might show a little more… Good gracious!"

Mr Pemberton-Oakes had seen it now, and in silence the two men stared at the fireplace where a small brass hook, weighted with a broken door-knob, was swinging gently to and fro like a noiseless pendulum.

For some seconds they watched, their eyes swivelling from left to right, like spectators at a tennis tournament. Then Mr Wilkins spoke.

"I… I… *Corwumph!*" he said.

"But what on earth is it?" queried the Headmaster.

"It's a small brass hook, weighted with a broken…"

"Yes, yes, yes, I can see that, Wilkins. But what's it doing in your fireplace? Is it some contraption you use for boiling kettles?"

"No, no, I assure you! I don't boil kettles. When I want a cup of tea I usually go next door to Matron's sitting-room. She often makes a pot of tea about…"

"Wilkins, this is hardly the moment to discuss your domestic arrangements," the Headmaster broke in. "Someone is up above on the flat roof. I suggest that you go and investigate forthwith."

"Yes, yes, of course." And Mr Wilkins charged away on his errand like a forward breaking loose from a rugger scrum. The door banged behind him with a force that dislodged a picture from above the mantelpiece and sent a current of air swirling about the Headmaster's ankles.

When the tumult had died away, Mr Pemberton-Oakes had another look at the fireplace, but the hook had disappeared. "Now, I wonder exactly what is happening up above," he asked himself.

Things had not been going well on the roof, and Jennings and Darbishire had been beset by difficulties from the moment of their arrival.

To begin with, not *one*, but a whole forest of chimneys stretched their necks into the fading light, and it was impossible to tell which one of them belonged to Mr Wilkins' study.

"It's hopeless," said Jennings. "We can't go dropping hooks down all of them. We'd better say, *eena meena mina mo* and hope for the best."

Darbishire had a better idea. "Mr Wilkins is bound to have lit his fire by now," he reported incorrectly. "So it must be one of those with smoke coming out."

Jennings clicked his tongue with impatience. "Don't be such a bogus coot, Darbi! If he *has* lit it, the smoke won't be coming up this way – it'll be back-firing all over his room. I vote we listen at all the ones without smoke and see if we can hear any coughing and spluttering coming up the spout."

They wasted precious minutes with their ears glued to the cowls, but no distress signals came from below. Finally, Jennings selected a chimney at random and dropped the weighted hook down inside.

"It's either this one or the next," he prophesied as the hook disappeared from view, "because Old Wilkie's room looks out over the quad and I...oh, gosh, Darbi! I've got a bite. There's something on the hook."

"Oh, wacko! First shot, too! Can you hoik it up?"

"I don't know. I'll have a try."

Jennings manoeuvred the hook round and round in the confined space, and presently his efforts were rewarded. He gave a gentle pull and felt the hook rising with its prize embedded on the end.

"I've got it! Wacko!" he cried, his eyes gleaming with triumph.

Darbishire danced happily amongst the chimney pots.

Success at the first attempt seemed too good to be true.

It was! And the dancer stopped in the middle of a wild cavort as the hook came to the surface dragging half a disused starling's nest with it.

"Oh, fish-hooks! It's only a bird's nest," Jennings snorted and the gleam of triumph went out of his eyes. "I ought to have guessed, really, because it was quite near the top and I couldn't have shoved the parcel all that way up."

He tried again, and this time the hook sank right down the well of the chimney as the line was paid out from above. Soon the string was stretched to its full length, but the weight had met no obstruction.

Disappointed, Jennings grunted: "Wrong chimney! It must be down to the fireplace by now. I can swing the hook from side to side quite easily, look."

"No good telling me to look," returned Darbishire. "I can't see what's going on down below."

But though Darbishire couldn't, Mr Wilkins *could!* For it was at that moment that he caught sight of the small brass hook floating gently into the fireplace, and lost the drift of the Headmaster's studied remarks.

Neither Jennings nor Darbishire had any idea of the keen interest with which their salvage operations were being followed on the floor below, and after half a minute of random twiddling, Jennings heaved on the line and the hook rose to chimney pot level,

"We'll try the next one," he said. "We've probably been fishing down Matron's sitting-room chimney, by mistake. Golly, wouldn't it have been awful if she'd seen the hook coming down!" He gave a little embarrassed laugh at the absurdity of such a happening.

As they moved to the neighbouring stack, it occurred to Jennings that he might be able to locate the right chimney by straining his eyes into the tunnel of darkness. If there was nothing in the way he should be able to see a pinpoint of light from the fireplace below. He pressed his face onto the rim of the next chimney and opened his eyes wide.

"Whatever are you doing now?" demanded Darbishire, impatiently.

"I'm peering into the darkness in the hope of seeing a light." The answer was not audible to Darbishire for it went straight down the chimney, which amplified the words like a megaphone and sent them booming out of the fireplace in the room below.

It was Matron's room; and she was pouring out a cup of tea when the voice of doom echoed hollowly down her chimney. Fortunately, her nerves were strong, but even so the sudden shock made her leap like a ballerina; the teapot danced in her unsteady grasp like a fire-hose out of control, sending a jet of hot tea into a potted plant on the sideboard.

When she recovered, she sat pondering over the message she had received from outer space! *Peering into the darkness in the hope of seeing a light!* It was as though some minor prophet were warning her of the shape of things to come.

Unaware of the havoc he had created below, Jennings raised his face from the chimney pot. "Can't see a thing," he announced.

"I can," Darbishire jerked out nervously. "I can see Mr Wilkins coming through the attic window, and he looks as though he's going into the attack at roof-top level."

Darbishire's fears were justified. Mr Wilkins swept over the flat roof like a ridge of high pressure approaching from Iceland. "I... I... *Corwumph!* What the... Why the... What are you two boys doing up here? You've no business to be on the roof. You know perfectly well it's out of bounds."

"Yes, sir."

They stood unhappily before him; Darbishire shock-headed as a dandelion, and Jennings with a thick black circle running right round his face, where Matron's chimney pot had left its mark.

"It strikes me you're going off your heads." stormed Mr Wilkins. "Of all the nonsensical buffoonery and thick skulled balderdash, I've ever come across, I've never seen anything to equal the stupidity of dangling guided missiles down flue-pipes, without rhyme or reason!" He paused for breath.

"I'm sorry, sir, but we weren't sure it *was* your chimney, sir," Jennings apologised. "We only – er, we only thought it *might* be."

"But you – you *silly* little boy, what do you want to put things down *anyone's* chimney for? You're not Father Christmas, are you!"

Mr Wilkins' voice rose to an exasperated squeak, and his hands seemed to be conducting an invisible orchestra as he groped for some shred of reason behind the fantastic absurdity of such behaviour.

"Well, sir, it was like this," Jennings explained. "We wanted to make sure that your chimney wasn't blocked, in case you decided to light your fire, sir."

"And why should you think that my chimney might be blocked?"

"They are sometimes, sir. And we were quite right as it happened, because we found this thing stuck in yours, sir."

Jennings picked up the crumbling bird's nest and held it out for the master's inspection.

Mr Wilkins looked at the bird's nest with distaste. It was an unpleasant object to have blocking up one's chimney and certain to have caused great inconvenience if it had not been removed before his fire was lighted.

"H'm!" said Mr Wilkins. The temperature of his indignation dropped a few degrees and he scratched his ear thoughtfully. Perhaps the silly little boys had meant well in their muddle-headed way; though why anyone in their senses should choose to play at chimney sweeps on draughty rooftops was more than he could imagine. Moreover, school rules could not be lightly broken for the sake of doing good turns, however praiseworthy the intentions were.

"Go downstairs at once," Mr Wilkins ordered. "And when you've washed your face, Jennings, I'll set you both some work to keep you out of mischief for the rest of the day."

In gloomy silence the boys climbed back through the attic window and went downstairs to the washroom, where Jennings soaped his face and transferred part of the sooty circle to the rim of the basin; the rest, he wiped off on the roller towel.

"I still don't see what's happened, Darbi," he said. "If that hook really went all the way down Wilkie's chimney, why didn't it collide with the fish-bag?"

"Search me," said Darbishire. "It's just one of those mysterious things no one can explain, like flying saucers and how they built Stonehenge."

The washroom had been empty when they had arrived, but now Venables sauntered in to remove the ink stains from his fingers before tea.

"I've been looking for you two characters," he began. "I've done you a supersonic favour."

"Thanks very much; that was decent of you," said Darbishire. "What was it?"

"Well, Matron wouldn't let me play football this afternoon because of my cold, so I thought it would be a good wheeze to snaffle that fish out of Old Wilkie's chimney while everyone was outside on the pitch."

"What!" Jennings spun round so violently that the towel came away from the wall and the roller thudded to the floor with a bang. "You mean to stand there and say it was *you* who took it?"

"Of course it was! I said at breakfast the other day that it shouldn't be too difficult. I'd have told you before only I couldn't find you. Where have you been?"

"Oh, nowhere special," said Darbishire in a flat, resigned voice. "We've only been up on the roof fishing for the beastly thing, with Old Wilkie going berserk and running amok round the chimney pots."

"Super sorrow; I thought you'd be jolly grateful."

"Oh we are! Please don't apologise. Next to having a picnic in a crocodile swamp, I can't think of a better way of spending a half holiday."

The parcel awaited them in Venables' tuck-box.

"I'm going to bury it directly after tea," Jennings decided. "I've just about had enough trouble over fish and I never want to look another one in the face again."

The tea bell ran and Venables smiled broadly as he turned to leave the room. "That's just where you're going to come unstuck, Jennings. I happen to know we're having kippers for tea this afternoon!"

7

Sponge Cake Substitute

The main purpose of the tuck-box room was, naturally enough, to provide storage space for tuck-boxes. It had not been designed as an editorial office, and Jennings and Darbishire had to carry out extensive alterations before they could set about marking the entries for the *Form Three Times* competitions.

First they piled up tuck-boxes to form a flat-topped desk, and then they pinned notices about the room. *Keep out – Strictly No Admission* was inscribed beneath the window; and in case this should seem rather forbidding, *Visitors Welcomed* hung from the lampshade and struck a kindlier note.

The magazine now boasted two suites of offices. The news department still had its headquarters in the hobbies room, but as this was neither quiet nor private, the editors had set up an annexe amongst the tuck-boxes, where competition entries could be studied without the competitors breathing down the judges' necks and trying to sway their decision.

By the following Friday week the entries had arrived, but the sponge cakes had not. This was serious, for the editor had publicly announced that he would present the prizes before tea on the following day.

"I can't think what's come over Aunt Angela," Jennings said, as he and Darbishire made for their private office after evening preparation. "It's over a week since I wrote and asked for those double-deckers. Mind you, I know she's as absent-minded as two coots, but you would think she'd try to remember, especially as I went to the trouble of underlining it in red ink."

Darbishire nodded. Aunt Angela's forgetfulness had caused chaos the previous term, when she had sent her nephew's postal order to the wrong address.

"People who are like that ought to do something about it," he said. "Like, say, for instance, tying knots in bits of string, so it reminds them to remember not to forget things?'

"You'd need something better than a bit of string for Aunt Angela," Jennings retorted. "She's so chronic she'd have to go round with a fifty-foot tow-rope full of clove hitches and bowlines before she'd remember everything." He shook his head sorrowfully. Absent-minded aunts ranked high amongst the problems of modern times to which there was no real answer.

There was still half an hour before bedtime as Jennings settled down at his editorial desk. He took a bundle of envelopes from his jacket pocket and passed them to his assistant.

"You sort the home-made poems from the best handwriters, and I'll use my indecision to pick out the winners. And we'll disqualify anyone who hasn't written *Comp* in the top left-hand corner."

Darbishire flicked through the little stack of envelopes, saying: "Comp, comp, comp," as he checked the observance of the rules. "Yes, they've all got it on…oh, wait a sec; here's one that hasn't." He peered in puzzled wonder at the writing on the envelope.

"Bung it in the waste-paper basket," was the editor's stern decision. "We can't have chaps forgetting simple instructions like that, or they'll grow up as scatterbrained as Aunt Angela."

"That's who this one's addressed to!" said Darbishire. "And, what's more, it's in your writing."

"What?"

"Look for yourself. *Miss Angela Birkinshaw*, as plain as a pikestaff."

He tore open the envelope and glanced at the contents: a passage underlined in red ink caught his eye:...*two double-decker jam sponge cakes, not less than approx. nine inches across, please.*

There was reproach in the assistant editor's pale blue eyes as he handed the letter to his chief. "You great, crumbling, addle-pated ruin, Jennings. You've forgotten to post it!"

Jennings stared at the letter in guilty dismay. "Oh, fish-hooks! If that isn't the rottenest bad luck," he complained. "I must have been carrying it round for days, and now it's got mixed up with the competition envelopes. I know I meant to post it because I can remember doing it."

"Don't be crazy! How could you have posted it, if here it is!"

"No, I mean I can remember *meaning* to post it. It's just hard cheese that I forgot."

"It's nothing of the sort. It's chronic absent-mindedness."

It was not often that Darbishire could criticise his friend without having to shoulder part of the blame himself. Now, however, he had a clear case, and could afford to let himself go without restraint.

"Of all the prehistoric clodpolls I ever met, you get the bronze medal for beetle-headedness," he said warmly. "There you sit, calmly wondering whether your aunt's memory has gone to seed, while all the time the letter's still cluttering up your pocket. My father says that people who..."

"Oh, shut up, Darbi! I may have made a bit of a bish, but you needn't go on tearing strips off about it all night. What we've got to think of now is what on earth we're going to do."

Jennings relapsed into a thoughtful silence, for the snags that lay ahead were only too obvious. The poets and the penmen had worked hard on the competitions, and if the advertised prizes were not forthcoming at the proper time there would be trouble. The reputation of the *Form Three Times* was at stake.

Presently Darbishire said: "I don't suppose the village shop would sell double-decker sponge cakes, but if we got permish to go into Dunhambury, we might get them there."

"And what do we use for money? I've spent all my cash on another film for the camera. How much have you got left?"

"About eight pence. It'd pay the fares all right, but there's not much point in going if we can't afford the cakes when we get there."

Jennings shrugged and said: "We'll think of something! Let's have a look at the comp entries first. If we're lucky they'll all be so ghastly that we shan't have to give any prizes at all. Wouldn't it be smashing if they were!"

It was an odd remark from one who had been hoping that the competition would reveal hidden talent, and it served to show how deeply the lack of prizes was preying on the editor's mind.

There were six envelopes marked *Comp*. The entry was smaller than they had been expecting, for many would-be competitors had dropped out of the running through lack of ideas or pressure of business. The editors were thankful now that the field had been narrowed. Even so, with no prizes to offer, six entries were still half a dozen too many.

Darbishire sorted out the sheets of paper and dropped the envelopes in the waste-paper basket. To his surprise, all six were poems. No one, it seemed, had entered for the handwriting prize after all.

"Well, that's a good thing," said Jennings. "If no one's gone in for it, that makes one sponge cake that we don't need."

"Yes, but who makes the other cake that we *do* need?" demanded the assistant editor.

"Let's not worry about that till we've seen whether the poems are mouldy or not. You read them out while I keep my fingers crossed and hope for the worst."

Darbishire glanced at the first manuscript. "This one's pretty ribby for a kick-off. It's Binns' famous effort." And he read aloud

" 'I am a pirate on the sea,
　　And I am most melan*cholee*.' "

"You're most *what?*" queried the chief editor.

"It isn't really melan*cholee*, but you have to say it like that to make it fit. It's – er – it's melancholy, I think. Yes, that's what it really is."

"Never mind what it really is. What is it *really?*"

"Melancholy? It means sad. Just like us if we can't think of a prize for... Well, I'd better get on, hadn't I?

" 'The crew are in a gloomy mood
　　Through being rather short of food.
　　For quite by chance I dropped their suppers
　　Through the scuppers...'

"That's enough of that one! Isn't it ghastly?"

"Frantic," Jennings agreed. "We needn't give a prize for that, anyway."

ANTHONY BUCKERIDGE

Darbishire continued to shake his head sadly over Binns' poetic shortcomings. "Now, if I'd been writing that poem, I should have written that last line a lot better. How would it be if I touched it up a bit by altering it to…"

"But, you radio-active clodpoll, Darbi, we don't *want* to make it better! The worse they are the less chance there is of having to give a prize that we haven't got."

"Sorry; I was forgetting." Darbishire picked up the next sheet and announced: "Cricket – by C A Temple.

"'You have to have a wicket
 Before you can play cricket.
 One day, we made 63 for 9,
 And the credit for this was all mine,
 The bowling was fast, but in spite of that
 Not an eyelid did I bat.'"

The assistant editor stopped reading and giggled. "Golly, isn't it feeble!"

"It's worse than that. All that stuff about his eyelids not batting doesn't even make sense," Jennings replied. "If he hadn't had his innings they might have written, *Temple – Did not Bat* in the scorebook. But they wouldn't put it about his eyelids, would they?"

"I don't think you quite understand," Darbishire explained. "It's what they call odi-itic – er – idio-matic, I should say."

Jennings did not argue the point. With two poems already rejected, the chances of having to award a prize were growing more remote; his only fear was that as the remaining poems could hardly be worse than the first two, they must be better. He stopped worrying, however, after hearing Bromwich's rhymed couplets on how to build a rabbit hutch. Atkinson's effort about a visit to the zoo was, if anything, worse; and

80

Thompson's poetic inspiration had ceased to flow after the first three lines, and his entry was rejected out of hand.

"That only leaves one more," said Jennings, as contribution number five slithered into the waste-paper basket. "Gosh, I do hope it's mouldy."

Darbishire glanced at the writing on the last sheet of paper and said: "This one's by Venables. Listen!

    " 'Break, break, break,
      On thy cold grey stones, O Sea!
    And I would that my tongue could utter
      The thoughts that arise in me.
    O well for the fisherman's boy,
      That he shouts with his sister at play!
    O well for the sailor lad,
      That he sings in his boat on the bay!' "

Jennings was deeply impressed. "Phew! That's not bad, is it! Who did you say wrote it?"

"Venables."

"He never did!"

"He must have done. That's Venables' writing; I'd know it anywhere. Not a blot on the whole page. Hang on, there's a bit more yet.

    " 'And the stately ships go on
      To their haven under the hill;
    But O for the touch of a vanish'd hand,
      And the sound of a voice that is still!

    Break, break, break,
      At the foot of thy crags, O Sea!
    But the tender grace of a day that is dead
      Will never come back to me.' "

There was a short silence. Then, rather grudgingly, Jennings said: "H'm! Well, his poem's certainly a lot better than the others. Mind you, I don't suppose Wordsworth and Tennyson and all that lot would think much of it, but it's not bad for a chap of twelve."

"That's what I was thinking," Darbishire answered. "We'll wizard well *have* to give him a prize for a super decent effort like that. Unless, of course, we can find something wrong with it."

But though they pored over the verses for some time, they were unable to make any serious criticisms. "There must be *something* the matter with it," Jennings argued. "What about the way he keeps on repeating 'O well'? He says 'O well for the fisherman's boy' and 'O well for the sailor lad.' People wouldn't really say that, would they?"

"Perhaps he couldn't think of anything else to put, so he just thought, 'O well,' and let it go at that."

Jennings frowned thoughtfully at the sheet of paper. "We can't disqualify it just because of that: somebody'll kick up a hoo-hah if we do. I suppose we'll just have to think of something else for a prize, that's all. If only I hadn't forgotten to post that letter!" He shook his head in self reproach. "Oh well, I suppose it can't be helped."

Darbishire looked up sharply. "There you are! You've just said it."

"Said what?"

" 'O well.' You said people wouldn't really say that."

The editor thumped his desk in exasperation. "Look here, Darbishire, what's the good of my trying to find something wrong if you keep cracking everything up to the skies and saying how marvellous it is?"

"Sorry, Jen. If you think it's rotten, don't give a prize."

"I *don't* think it's rotten. It's supersonic, and I'd give him a sponge cake like a shot, if only I'd got one to give. Let's think what we could dish him out with instead."

No word was spoken for some minutes as the editors paced to and fro among the tuck-boxes, racking their brains until they ached. But neither of them could think of a prize which was not immediately vetoed by the other. Darbishire's proposal that Jennings should award his camera was met with an indignant refusal: and Jennings' suggestion of Darbishire's four-bladed penknife led to a bitter and fruitless argument.

The discussion was interrupted by the ringing of the dormitory bell and the boys went up to bed with the problem unsolved. As they undressed, they were surrounded by the unsuccessful competitors demanding to know how they had fared.

"Have you marked those poems yet?" shrilled Binns, twirling his socks before his face like contra-rotating propellors.

"Yes. There was only one decent one," Jennings replied.

"Mine?"

"No. Yours went into the waste-paper basket."

"Oh!" The propellers stopped whirling and Binns turned away, as gloomy as the melancholy pirate of his imagination. He had spent a lot of time on that poem.

"What about mine?" queried Temple.

"Yours was pretty feeble, too," said Jennings. "I shouldn't really tell you who's the winner, because it's still on the secret list, but if you promise not to spread it, I don't mind saying that Venables' effort was a smasher."

"Good old Ven!" cried Temple generously; and unmindful of official secrets, he shouted down the dormitory: "Hey, Venables, you've won first prize in the wall-paper comp."

83

Venables raised a partly-washed face from the basin. "Have I? Oh, wacko!" he exclaimed, and came hurrying along, showering a spray of soap bubbles over everyone in his path. "When do I get the sponge cake?" he demanded.

The editor seemed not to hear, and the question was repeated. Then he said: "Well, there's been a bit of a bish over that. There aren't any going just at present."

"What! You mouldy swizzler, Jennings! I demand a prize! You promised it!" Venables' sense of fair play was outraged; and indeed the whole dormitory was stirred by such rank injustice.

"You can't get away with that, Jennings! You could be had up for fraudulent confidence tricks," said Atkinson.

"If I don't get my prize, there's going to be some bashing-up going on round these parts," threatened the angry winner: he was far too indignant to notice the uncomfortable trickles of water coursing down his chest.

"All right, all *right*. Don't get in a flap. You'll get your prize; don't you worry!"

"Double-decker sponge cake?"

"No; something better. Something ten times better! It's a secret till the prize-giving tomorrow, but I guarantee you'll like it."

These were wild statements, and Jennings knew it; but the reputation of the *Form Three Times* was at stake, and no other course was open to him.

Reassured, Venables returned to his washing and the crowd faded away from Jennings' bed. When they had gone Darbishire said: "I'm jolly glad you've thought of something. Jen. What is it?"

"I don't know, yet."

"But you just said... Oh, fish-hooks!" His friend's announcement had sounded so convincing that Darbishire was sure some bright idea must have occurred to him. Now, it seemed, the editors would be branded as unscrupulous confidence tricksters – to say nothing of the threatened violence which would have to be faced if Venables' demands were not met. Moreover, the prize must be something worth having. It would be asking for trouble to foist some worthless object on a winner who was looking forward to something ten times better than double-decker sponge cake.

"Couldn't we sell something, and buy something else with the money?" Darbishire spoke in low tones so that none but Jennings might hear.

"I'm not parting with my camera or my printing set, thanks very much."

"No, I mean some old relic that's worth a lot just because it's ancient. If only we'd got something like that! You'd be surprised how much antiques and things are worth. My father knows a man who's got a book written by some old geezer round about Julius Caesar's time, and he says it's worth about a hundred pounds."

"Who says – Julius Caesar?"

"No, you clodpoll! My father says. It's a rare first edition, you see."

"What's the good of telling me all this? I haven't got anything written about Julius Caesar's time. Except, of course, my Latin book. They're always saying what sort of a time he had, in that."

"Oh no, that's no good at all. I'm talking about valuable first editions that collectors go in for when they're about a hundred years old – the books, I mean – not the collectors."

"I bet my Latin book's not far short of a hundred, anyway," Jennings maintained. "It's terribly dog-eared; and what's more, I'm pretty sure it's got 'first edition' printed inside. There are only about two like it in the whole school; apart from me and Venables, everyone else has got much newer ones."

"Don't be a coot, Jennings! You're not going to tell me that your Latin book is really valuable!"

Jennings' voice rose in exasperation. "But you great bazooka, Darbi – it was you who just said it *was!* When I thought I hadn't got an ancient priceless book, you told me how rare they were. Now I find I *have* got one you tell me they're no good. Make your mind up, for goodness' sake! You can't have it both ways!"

Darbishire didn't want it both ways. Nothing would have pleased him more than to discover that Jennings' Latin book was as valuable as the mouldering tome belonging to his father's friend. He knew that *Grimshaw's Latin Grammar* was in short supply for there were not enough copies to go round the class; and if Jennings really *did* own a first edition…! "Go and fetch it, Jen. We might be able to find out, if we examine it closely."

It was nearly time for the dormitory lights to be put out, but Jennings was willing to risk the master-on-duty's wrath when such an important issue was at stake. Quietly, he slipped out of the dormitory and down the stairs to his classroom.

A few moments ticked by while he rummaged in his untidy desk; somehow the larger books always seemed to rise to the top, and leave the smaller ones in a muddled heap below. But at last he found it. *A First Latin Grammar by Arnold Grimshaw, MA, DLitt. Late Lecturer in Classical Studies in the University of Oxbridge. First Edition MCMLII.*

Jennings furrowed his brow as he strove to translate the Roman numerals. *MCMLII.* That must be… Er – um… Yes, of course: 1852!

Holding the precious volume more carefully than usual, he slammed down his desk-lid and scampered back to his dormitory. As he ran, his mind was busy working out a plan of campaign. First he must find out, upon good authority, if the book was as valuable as the evidence suggested. If it was, he would sell it for – well, Darbishire had mentioned a hundred pounds as a likely figure; but even if it produces rather less – say about fifty pence, for instance – there would still be enough to buy Venables his sponge cake and leave some over for a modern edition of the book at the published price of twenty-five pence. This part of the scheme was most important; for though the book was his to dispose of, his imagination boggled at what the Headmaster would say if he arrived in class without one. Why, if the Head ever got to hear of...

Jennings stopped dead in his tracks, for the object of his thoughts was standing at the top of the stairs, regarding him with the look which he reserved for boys who were discovered out of their dormitory after lights out.

"Come here, Jennings," said Mr Pemberton-Oakes.

It was too late to conceal the Latin book; and with an empty feeling inside him, Jennings realised that Question Time was about to begin.

"Are you aware, Jennings, that your dormitory light was put out nearly five minutes ago?"

Jennings fumbled with his dressing-gown cord and answered with a low buzzing noise which could have meant either "Yes sir" or "No sir."

"Then I am somewhat at a loss to understand, Jennings, why you are not in bed."

"I just slipped down to my classroom to get a book, sir."

Mr Pemberton-Oakes raised one eyebrow. He held strong views about reading under the bedclothes by torchlight.

"And how, may I ask, do you propose to read in total darkness?" But at that moment he caught sight of the book which Jennings was holding, and his expression changed. "*Grimshaw's Latin Grammar*, eh! Well, well, Jennings, I must confess that I am surprised at your choice of bedtime reading. Does this indicate that you are at last proposing to take the subject seriously?"

Jennings smiled modestly. "Oh, I don't know, sir. I just thought I'd have a look through it before lights out if there was time. Or perhaps in the morning, before I get up, sir."

The Headmaster nodded approvingly. He had misjudged the boy. Admittedly, his work had not shown much promise so far, but if he was willing to pursue his studies in his free time, there was still hope of improvement.

"I congratulate you, Jennings. You have left it too late for this evening, but I can imagine no better way of starting tomorrow than by putting in ten minutes' concentrated revision of *Grimshaw's Grammar*. A most invaluable book."

"Thank you, sir." It seemed a good moment to obtain an expert opinion. "Would you say it was very rare, sir?"

"It's almost unobtainable, if that's what you mean. I've had copies on order for months," the Headmaster replied. "A very interesting man – Dr Grimshaw. I used to attend his lectures at the university."

Jennings opened his eyes wide in astonishment. "You – you've actually seen him, sir?"

"Frequently."

Jennings continued to gape. At that rate, Dr Grimshaw must be about a hundred and fifty years old. No wonder he was interesting!

"It says here, sir," he pointed out politely, "that he wrote this book in 1852."

Mr Pemberton-Oakes glanced at the title page. "No, Jennings. *MCMLII* is – well, work it out for yourself. A mental revision of Roman numerals will do you no harm before you drop off to sleep. Good night!"

He hummed softly to himself as he strode off down the landing. It was most gratifying that his patient efforts to interest the boy in Latin were now beginning to bear fruit – most gratifying! Of course it was stupid of him to make a mistake of a hundred years in translating the Roman numerals, but a little concentrated revision would soon put that right.

Jennings hurried into his dormitory and groped his way to his bed, to find Darbishire anxiously awaiting his return.

"Have you got it, Jennings?" he breathed in the hissing, voiceless whisper he used after silence had been called.

"Yes. And you're quite right. The Archbeako says it's as priceless as coots' eggs."

"Golly! The Head actually said that?"

"He used different words, but that's what he meant. Here you are; see for yourself."

Darbishire stretched into the darkness and his hand closed upon the precious volume. Then he burrowed headfirst down his bed and switched on his torch. From without, a pale, ghostly haze could be seen shimmering round the bed, as though the blankets were phosphorescent.

Very carefully Darbishire studied the pages. They were yellow and musty: which was not to be wondered at, for Jennings had left the book out all night in a thunderstorm. But to Darbishire's unpractised eye the discoloured markings were proof of old age. He spent some time poring over the author's qualifications on the title page, and then he switched off his torch and crawled back to the surface where the air was fresher. His untucked bedclothes gave him some trouble for the rest of the night.

"It's a rare first edition, all right," he confided to Jennings in a whisper. "I don't suppose it's as valuable as my father's friend's antique geezer's book is, but it's bound to be worth something. All really old books are."

Jennings raised his head from his pillow. "We were wrong about that. The Archbeako seemed to think it was quite modern."

"He must be stark raving bats! Anyone can see how old it is, and what's more the author's dead, so that proves it."

"How do you know he's dead?"

"It says so in the book. It calls him a *Late Lecturer*."

"That's nothing to go by. It probably means he's never on time for his lectures."

"I bet you it doesn't!" Darbishire maintained. "I bet you a million pounds that 'late' means dead. I read in the paper once about a chap called the late Mr Somebody-or-other and it turned out he'd been dead for years."

Jennings wasn't convinced. "But how can this book have been written by a dead man?"

"Well, perhaps he wasn't dead when he wrote it, but he is now," came the logical answer.

"Have it your own way; it isn't worth arguing about. The point is that whether he's alive or not, I've got the Head's word of honour that the book's invaluable. So first thing tomorrow, we'll decide how we can sell it for a lot of money."

They fell silent then, and in the few minutes before he dropped asleep, Jennings' mind was picturing wealthy collectors bidding frantically against one another for possession of the late lecturer's contribution to classical studies. It was kind of Fate, he thought, to point such a clear way out of their difficulties.

8

The Brilliant Forgery

Ideas which seem brilliant at bedtime often lose their appeal when reviewed in the clear light of morning: cracks appear in the structure of flawless plans, and damp patches seep through the joints of watertight schemes.

Thus it was that, as Jennings stirred his breakfast tea on the following morning, his high hopes of the night before dissolved as swiftly as the sugar in his cup.

To begin with, there was no second-hand bookshop nearer than the market town of Dunhambury, and Mr Carter would never give them permission to make so long a journey. And even supposing they reached Dunhambury, would they be able to find a bookseller willing to pay anything from fifty pence to a hundred pounds for the works of A Grimshaw, DLitt? It seemed extremely unlikely.

He was about to confide his doubts to Darbishire, when Venables spoke from across the table.

"You'd better not forget my prize, Jennings. It's got to be something good, too, or else..." And he narrowed his eyes and sliced off the top of his egg with gestures full of meaning.

"Yes, what's it going to be?" demanded Atkinson.

Jennings looked thoughtful. "I can't tell you yet, because" – he might as well admit it – "well, because I haven't got it yet."

And as a storm of protest rose from across the table, he added quickly: "But it's all right. I'm going to sell my Latin book and buy something with the money."

"Sell your Latin book!" The table was aghast. Eyebrows shot up like window-blinds, and mouths which had opened to receive spoonfuls of egg remained ajar in sheer astonishment.

"Yes, as a matter of fact I happen to know it's worth quite a bit. It's a genuine first edition, you see."

"But what will you use in class?"

"Oh, that's all right. The Archbeako won't know, because I shall buy a later model of the same make."

The words were thrown out casually, and only Jennings knew the uncertainty that lay behind them. But there could be no going back now; there would be a dozen witnesses to speak against him if he failed in his quest.

There was no football fixture that Saturday, and village leave was granted after lunch. That meant that the boys might go as far as the village and buy sweets at the *Linbury Stores and Post Office* or doughnuts and ginger pop at the little cottage with the notice in the window: *Chas Lumley – Home-made Cakes and Bicycles Repaired*. But Jennings and Darbishire had other plans.

After lunch, they gave in their names to Mr Carter and set off down the drive; but before they had reached the gates there was a pounding of footsteps behind them, and Venables came rushing to catch them up. In his hand he carried a copy of *Grimshaw's Latin Grammar*.

"Hang on a sec," he panted, as he drew level. "Are you characters *really* going to Dunhambury?"

"Ssh! Don't broadcast it," hissed Jennings. "If Mr Carter finds out we're going farther than Linbury village there'll be the most supersonic hoo-hah."

Venables looked up and down the drive to make sure they were unobserved. Then he said: "It's about these Latin books.

Mine's a first edition, too, so I wondered if you'd mind taking it along with yours."

"I wouldn't sell yours if I were you," Darbishire advised. "Jen's only sacrificing his because of the sponge cake famine."

"Oh, go on; be decent!"

Jennings considered. It would be just as easy to dispose of two volumes as it would be to sell a single copy, if the Headmaster's word was to be trusted. "All right; bung it over," he agreed.

"Coo, super thanks," grinned Venables. "There's just one thing, though. Make sure you can buy a cheaper edition before you get rid of the rare one. The Archbeako will go berserk if I haven't got a book for his class on Monday."

Jennings and Darbishire hurried down the drive and turned out of the school gates. There was a Request Stop some fifty yards along the road, but it would be risky to board a bus so near the school premises, so they made for the fare stage round the corner.

Time was short, for Dunhambury lay some five miles to the west and they were due to report back to school by half-past four. For quarter of an hour they waited by the bus stop, flipping their fingers with impatience as the precious minutes ticked by. At last a single decker bus appeared round the bend and stopped in answer to their frenzied waving.

The journey to Dunhambury was uneventful. Darbishire bought the tickets and made a note in his diary to claim his expenses if the expedition should prove successful. Twenty minutes later they were picking their way through the Saturday afternoon shopping crowds and looking with a desperate urgency for a second-hand bookshop.

"Oh, fish-hooks, this is feeble," lamented Darbishire, after they had wandered the length of the main street without success. "It's all ironmongers and corn-chandlers along here."

"There must be one somewhere," Jennings urged. "Unless they're all too busy mongering iron and chandling corn to have any time over for books around these parts."

"Shall we ask?"

"Whether they're too busy to read?"

"No, you clodpoll! Shall we ask where a shop is?"

"Better not. This is a top priority secret mission, don't forget, and we don't want everyone to…" Jennings stopped and looked at his friend oddly. "You crazy maniac, Darbi, what have you still got your school cap on for? Do you want everyone to know?"

"Oh, sorry." Darbishire snatched off the offending garment and stuffed it in his pocket.

They turned down a side street, past garages and greengrocers and little cafés; and they were beginning to despair of finding what they wanted, when Jennings came to a sudden halt and pointed hopefully at a small shop on the other side of the road.

"Look, Darbi. Over there! It's just the sort of place, isn't it!"

Darbishire looked. "Golly, yes! Masses of ancient, prehistoric books! I shouldn't be surprised if some of them go right back to William Caxton's time."

They hurried across the road for a closer inspection of the premises.

Thos. Barlow – Bookseller was inscribed in faded gilt letters above the shop front. Books were heaped untidily in the window, but it was so long since the glass had been cleaned that it was impossible to read their titles. Outside on the pavement, more volumes were stacked on an unsteady trestle-table.

"Pretty risky, leaving these out in the street," Darbishire remarked. "They might be valuable first editions, like my father's friend's priceless old relic."

Jennings removed a well-thumbed copy of the *Complete Works of Alfred, Lord Tennyson* from the top of the pile and blew the dust off its covers.

"I should think this one must be pretty expensive – it's fat enough," he observed. "Half a mo – it's got the price inside."

"A hundred pounds?" queried Darbishire hopefully.

"No, ten pence. Perhaps it's only a second edition, though. Let's go in, shall we!"

It was a dark little shop, and just for a moment they thought it was empty: for Thomas Barlow, bookseller, was a man who matched his surroundings so closely that he might have been camouflaged to tone with his dingy background. Standing there behind the counter, he seemed as faded as the gilt lettering above his door; his clothes were as dusty and dog-eared as the books on his shelves, and he peered at his customers through spectacles no cleaner than his plate-glass window.

"Well?" he inquired in a high-pitched croak.

Jennings handed him the two copies of the book he carried. "How much would these be worth, please?" he asked anxiously.

Mr Barlow pushed his spectacles onto his forehead so that he could see more clearly.

"H'm. *Grimshaw's First Latin Grammar*. Ah, yes, a very good book, this. Worth its weight in gold."

He flicked through the pages and seemed not to notice the frequent ink and finger stains and the occasional missing page. "Very good condition, they are. Beautiful binding," he assured them.

"You really think so? Oh, wacko! D'you hear that, Darbi! We're in the money, this time." Jennings turned back to the counter. "How much, then, please?" he asked.

Mr Barlow pursed his lips and looked up at the ceiling. "Let's say twenty-five pence each, shall we?"

"Oh! Is that all?" Jennings could not keep the disappointment out of his voice. Twenty-five pence seemed a far cry from a hundred pounds. Why, it was barely enough to buy copies of the cheaper edition and left practically nothing for Venables' prize.

"They're a bargain at the price," wheezed Mr Barlow. "You wouldn't buy them cheaper than that, anywhere."

"*Buy* them! But I don't want to buy them – I want to *sell* them," Jennings insisted.

The bookseller's gaze came down from the ceiling and he looked at his customers sharply. "Let me get this straight," he said. "Didn't you get these books from that table outside my shop?"

"Heavens, no! We brought them with us. They're ours – really they are!"

"How do I know you're speaking the truth?" came the unexpected reply. "I've been caught that way before. People bring me in a book and I give them a good price for it, and all the time it's my own property they've picked up outside the door. I fetched a policeman to the last one I caught playing that game."

"Oh, but honestly, we're not playing any game. You must believe us!" Jennings' tone was urgent. The situation was delicate enough as it was; if the police were called in, there was no knowing where the whole miserable fiasco would end. He began to wish they had never embarked on the scheme. Ever since breakfast that morning his enthusiasm had been cooling: now it had become ice-bound.

But apparently the bookseller was satisfied with his customer's answer, for he picked up the volumes again and grunted: "These books aren't much good to me. Been knocked about too much. Pages missing and what-all."

"But you just said what good condition they were in," Darbishire pointed out.

"M'yes, but that was before I knew you wanted to *sell* them. Tell you what – I'll give you two pence each for them."

"Two pence! Gosh, that's a swindle!" Jennings felt suddenly angry. "They were worth twenty-five *p* each a minute ago when you thought we wanted to buy them."

Mr Barlow arched his eyebrows and the movement sent his glasses slithering down onto his nose again.

"That's business, sonny," he explained in his husky croak. "These old copies aren't worth…. Hey, just a moment! I had someone in asking for *Grimshaw's Grammar* not so long ago. If I've got a customer waiting, I might see my way to…" His voice trailed off as he searched beneath the counter for his order book. Soon his head came into view once more and a parched smile was spread thinly across his face.

"Yes, I thought so! The Headmaster of Linbury Court Preparatory School asked me to send him any copies I came across."

He seized the two volumes and planked two coins down on the counter. "Five pence each, I'm giving you. You can't want fairer than that, eh!"

Jennings and Darbishire stared at Mr Barlow in horrified dismay. Their minds reeled at the thought of Mr Pemberton-Oakes paying twenty-five pence for a book which he fondly believed to be in Jennings' desk. Why, they couldn't have accepted a hundred pounds a volume in circumstances like that!

"I – I don't want to sell them. I want them back," Jennings jerked out.

But Mr Barlow now seemed reluctant to part with them. "You won't get a better price anywhere else. Robbing myself, that's what I'm doing. Tell you what, I'll make it fifteen pence for the two of them."

"No, really, thanks. They're not for sale."

"Not for sale! What d'you mean, not for sale? You just said that's what you'd come in here for."

"Yes, I know, but I've decided to change my mind quite suddenly."

With very bad grace the bookseller pushed the books across the counter and pocketed his coins.

"Strikes me you need your heads seeing to; coming in here, wasting my time and not knowing whether you want to buy books, or sell them. Go on, get out of my shop, and take your books with you!"

They were only too glad to go!

Once outside the door, Darbishire said: "Phew! That was a near-miss, wasn't it! I can just imagine the Archbeako buying those books and finding your name inside." The very thought of it was so shattering that he leaned heavily on Mr Barlow's trestle-table while he recovered from the shock.

Unfortunately, the table made a poor shock-absorber. There was a sudden movement from beneath as the trestles collapsed and the stack of books thudded to the pavement.

"You clumsy clodpoll! Now look what you've done!" barked Jennings.

"Sorry, Jen! It was that stupid table. I only touched it ever so…"

"Quick; pile them up before the old codger comes out of his shop! I've had enough of him to be going on with."

Hurriedly they replaced the fallen trestles and stooped to gather up the books. Luckily, Mr Barlow had not heard the crash and remained in his shop unaware of what had happened.

"Put them back tidily," said Jennings, as he retrieved the *Complete Works of Alfred, Lord Tennyson* from a puddle in the gutter. The volume was streaked with mud and had to be dry-cleaned with a handkerchief.

Carefully, Jennings inspected the pages for signs of damage. "There! I think it's all right now, so we'll just put it…" He broke off and stared in surprise at the printed page before him.

"What's the matter?" asked Darbishire anxiously.

"Gosh, Darbi! Golly! What do you think I've found?"

"A priceless prehistoric book-mark?"

"No, nothing like that. Listen to this on page 134 of Tennyson's poems:

" 'Break, break, break,
    On thy cold grey stones, O Sea!
  And I would that my tongue could utter
    The thoughts that arise in me.' "

"Yes, it *is* rather lovely, isn't it!" said Darbishire with deep appreciation. "You know, Jen, I think I've heard that poem before, somewhere."

"I should jolly well think you *have*," cried Jennings. "The next verse goes on: 'O well for the fisherman's boy.' "

Darbishire had placed it by this time. "That's right! Of course! It's Venables' famous prize poem."

"It jolly well isn't! It's Tennyson's. It's in his book, so that proves it!" His voice rose excitedly. "You see what this means, Darbi? We've been made the victims of a brilliant forgery. Venables never wrote this poem – he stole it from Lord Alfred Tennyson!"

Darbishire's expression was thoughtful. "I think it's the other way about," he observed.

"What! You mean Lord Alfred pinched it from Venables?"

"No, I mean you've got the name the wrong way round. You should say Alfred, Lord – not Lord Alfred. My father says that if a chap inherits a title…"

Jennings turned on his friend impatiently. "Don't quibble, Darbishire! We've been swizzled! We've got proof here of the dirty works of Venables in the complete works of Tennyson. Gosh, what a mouldy cad Venables is, pinching Alfred Lord's poem like that. Why, it's enough to make him turn in his grave."

They replaced the book tidily and hurried off to catch the bus. Jennings was smouldering with indignation. It was as though the mud he had wiped from the second-hand volume now besmirched the fair name of Venables. Let him talk his way out of *that*, if he could!

The only consolation was that as the winning poem was now disqualified, the editors would not have to present a prize after all: which was just as well, as they had no prize to present.

"What a ghastly bish it all is," lamented Darbishire, as they stood by the bus stop. "And it was such a lovely poem too." Dreamily, he recited:

" 'And I would that my tongue could utter
The thoughts that arise in me.' "

Jennings snorted angrily. It was clear that *his* tongue would have no difficulty in uttering the thoughts that arose in him the next time he met Venables.

9

Jennings Presents the Prize

At the moment when Jennings and Darbishire were boarding the four o'clock bus for their return journey, Venables was trotting light-heartedly across the quad, unaware of the serious charge he would be called upon to answer. He hummed gaily as he made his way into the building and upstairs to Mr Carter's room.

"Please, sir, I'm back from the village, sir. Will you tick me off on the list, please."

Mr Carter did so and said: "If you're going along to the common room, Venables, you can pin this notice on the board for me."

"Certainly, sir." Venables took the sheet of paper and glanced at it. *There will be an inspection of all text-books at 5 p.m. this afternoon*, it said.

Suddenly, he felt uneasy. Why this sudden interest in text-books, he wondered? Supposing Jennings had let him down! Supposing he did not return in time! Worst of all, supposing he had sold the valuable first editions and had then been unable to buy any cheaper copies!

Anxiously, he asked: "Why are we having an inspection sir?"

"It's time we made a check," Mr Carter replied. "There's a shortage of Latin grammars and the Head wants to find out how many are missing"

A shortage of Latin grammars! Venables shuffled his feet nervously. If Jennings had bungled things, the shortage was going to be uncomfortably acute!

"Are they difficult to get, sir? The cheaper editions I mean."

"Practically impossible," said Mr Carter. "I think they must be out of print at the moment."

Venables went downstairs seriously perturbed. He was a boy who believed in steering clear of trouble, and he bitterly regretted his rashness in having had anything to do with the scheme at all. Why, oh why, had he entrusted his book to Jennings? No longer could he look forward to receiving his prize with an easy mind. In fact, he no longer cared about the prize at all: but he *did* care about his Latin book!

In the common room he found Temple and Atkinson glancing through the *Form Three Times*.

"It's about time they got cracking on the next copy." Temple was saying. "This ancient old ruin will be growing whiskers if it stays up much longer."

"Give them a chance! There's a lot of work in printing a magazine, don't forget. I expect Jennings is just waiting for some more news to happen."

They made way for Venables to pin up the notice, which they read without much interest. Book inspections were nothing to get excited about – provided that the books were there to be inspected.

Worried and anxious, Venables told them what had happened.

"…and he was going to sell it and buy me a cheaper one, and now this mouldy inspection's coming off to bish up the whole issue," he finished miserably.

"I shouldn't worry. You'll get your second edition one as soon as Jennings gets back," said Temple.

"But I shan't! Mr Carter says you can't buy them any more, and Jennings is bound to have sold the old ones before he finds out. It's just the sort of thing he *would* do."

"It's your own crazy fault for giving it to him," was Atkinson's verdict. "I've told you fifty million times that Jennings' mighty famous wheezes always come unstuck." He shook his head sadly. "It's no good giving you good advice, Venables; it just goes in one ear and out of the other like water off a duck's back."

"Oh, don't talk such antiseptic eyewash, Atki," said Venables, testily. "What's my Latin grammar got to do with a duck's back, anyway?"

"It's just a saying. Everyone knows that if you pour water on a duck's back, it runs off."

"I don't blame it," said Temple. "So would anyone if you did that to them."

"I don't mean the duck runs off – I mean the water does." Atkinson explained impatiently. "Anyway, let this be a lesson to you, Venables. I reckon it'll be curtains for you at five o'clock."

"Huh! *And* for Jennings – I'll tell him a thing or two," threatened Venables. "Just wait till he gets back, that's all. Just you wait!"

They waited for twenty minutes. Then the common room door burst open and Jennings and Darbishire stood panting on the threshold. They had run all the way up the drive, but Jennings still had enough breath left to deliver himself of a few well-chosen words.

"So there you are, Venables, you miserable specimen! You'll be pleased to know you're a mouldy swizzler and a rotten bogus cheat. We've caught you red-handed in the act, and don't try to deny it, or you'll get your chips!"

The threats were wasted on Venables. "Thank goodness you've come back, Jen. Quick, have you got my Latin book?"

"Never mind about Latin books. You're a thief! You've stolen Lord Alfred's works."

The little crowd which had been gathering in the common room pricked up its ears.

"Stolen Alfred's works!" echoed Temple blankly. Who on earth was Alfred? he wondered. It sounded like a grandfather clock or an engine of some sort.

Darbishire pushed his way through the crowd, waving a sheet of paper which he had retrieved from the tuck-box room, on his way upstairs.

"Proof! Proof!" he shouted dramatically, and held the vital evidence two inches from the defendant's nose. "You see this, Venables, with *Break, Break, Break*, on it?"

Venables nodded. He could hardly avoid seeing it at such close range.

"You don't deny it's your writing, do you?"

"No, of course I don't," replied Venables. "It's the one I sent in for the competition."

"Well, it *isn't* your writing! It's Alfred, Lord Tennyson's," Jennings announced in firm tones.

Venables looked at him in amazement. "You're cuckoo! D'you think I don't know my own writing?"

The interested spectators were well out of their depth by this time, and Darbishire did his best to make matters plain.

"No, listen; we know it's Venables' writing, but we've found out that he didn't make the poem up and Tennyson did – which proves he's a fraudulent forger. What have you got to say about that, Venables, old boy?"

The common room buzzed with excitement. Fraudulent forgeries were not discovered every day of the week! All eyes were on Venables, and the excited buzz died away as he opened his mouth to speak.

"But I didn't send it in for the *home-made poetry* section," he said. "I sent it in for the *best handwriting* comp. The rules said you'd got to write about twenty lines, so I copied this poem out of a book. I never pretended I'd made it up myself."

Jennings' jaw dropped slightly. This, then, was the explanation. He could have kicked himself for not having thought of it. Avoiding his co-editor's eye, he mumbled: "Oh! H'm! Yes, I see." And to bolster up his tottering prestige, he added: "Yes, but how were we to know which one you meant it for? You should have said which one it was on the back."

"I couldn't do that. The rules said write on one side only," Venables explained. "If you don't believe me, take a squint at the envelope. That'll tell you plainly enough!"

The editors, accompanied by the prize-winner and the entire crowd of interested spectators, descended to the tuck-box room where, from the depths of the waste-paper basket, Darbishire produced the missing envelope. In addition to the name of the sender, it bore the words *Handwriting Comp.* in the top left-hand corner.

"Sorry, Jen," said Darbishire humbly. "I must have overlooked it in the heat of the moment."

"Yes, and what about his prize?" demanded Temple. "You promised it before tea, don't forget, so you'd better get weaving and hand it over."

The prize! In the light of this fresh evidence something would have to be done. For there could be no denying that Venables' handwriting was neat and legible, and as the only entrant in that section he was entitled to have his labours rewarded.

But with *what*? Jennings gave it up in despair. He had solved a whole series of difficult problems only to find himself back where he started. He took a deep breath and said: "Well, it's like this; we *were* going to get you a double-decker sponge cake with the cash we got for the Latin books, but..."

"Oh, golly!" Venables exclaimed, with a start. He had forgotten all about his Latin book in the hectic argument of the last ten minutes. That wretched book inspection would be starting at any moment, and there was Jennings calmly talking about the money he had obtained for the precious volume.

"You're a rotter, Jennings!" he burst out angrily. "You can keep your mouldy double-deckers, I don't want them! All I want is my Latin book back."

A tiny ray of hope was switched on in Jennings' heart.

"More than anything else?" he asked,

"Yes. It's the only thing I *do* want; but if you've sold it, what's the good of arguing?"

Jennings climbed up on a tuck-box and beckoned to the interested spectators. "Gather round, everybody!" he called loudly. "The *Form Three Times* famous handwriting prize is now going to be publicly presented to the lucky winner."

"I don't *want* a prize. I want my Latin book back," complained the lucky winner. But his protests were lost in the volume of applause which greeted the announcement.

When it had ceased, Jennings began his speech.

"Ladies and Gentlemen – er, no, cut out the ladies – Gentlemen and others! I am very proud at being asked to come here this afternoon to tell you – er, that I am very proud to come here."

"Hear, hear!" said Darbishire, trying his hardest to sound equally full of pride.

"Get a shift on; it'll be five o'clock soon," said Bromwich.

"All right; don't get impatient." The speaker cleared his throat. "Instead of a supersonic double-decker jam sponge cake, as advertised, the first and only prize will be this – er, this valuable prize, which I bet the winning character will like ten times better."

Venables had been listening without much interest; but now his heart missed a beat, for Jennings had taken two copies of *Grimshaw's Grammar* from his pocket and was solemnly holding one of them out towards its rightful owner.

"Oh, wacko!" yelled the prize-winner, as he grabbed the book and danced round the tuck-boxes with heartfelt relief. "So you didn't sell it, after all!"

After that there were solemn hand-shakings, for Jennings felt that he should conclude the ceremony in the formal manner of the distinguished visitors who presented the school prizes on Speech Day. On those occasions the speaker always wound up his remarks with some apt quotation from the classics. Perhaps he could do the same.

Assuming a pompous, speech-day manner, he said: "Finally, then, gentlemen, I would ask you to remember the valuable words of the late Dr Grimshaw which he has expressed so well in his priceless book, '*Amo, amas, amat, amamus, amatis, amant!*'."

But the prize-winner was not listening to the sound advice. He was hurrying through the door, hoping to be first in the queue for the five o'clock book inspection.

The wise sayings of Darbishire's father were well-known – and equally well ignored – throughout the school. At times of crisis *My father says…*was sure to be followed by some words of wisdom advising patience, courage, caution or hope to suit the occasion. And now that the prize-giving ceremony had been such a success, Darbishire lost no time in hammering home the need to press on with the next number of their magazine.

His father's stock of action proverbs came in useful for this, and during the next few days Jennings was continually urged to take bulls by the horns and strike irons while hot. Time and Tide, it appeared, were positively churlish about being kept waiting.

"That's all very well," said Jennings during hobbies hour the following Monday, "but we're a bit up a gum-tree for news at the moment. That's the trouble with boarding school – you never get anything decent happening, like revolutions and earthquakes and crime waves and things. It seems a bit feeble to have big headlines about Bromwich winning the Form Three ping-pong championship, but we'll have to make do with it, if we can't find anything else."

"And I vote we don't have any competitions this time," Darbishire advised. "They're too much strain on the nerves. Besides, we can't go *on* giving chaps their own property back as prizes or they'll think it a bit odd."

It was Jennings who suggested making a special feature of the 2nd XI "away" match against Bracebridge School. The game was fixed for the following Saturday, and as it involved a journey by bus and train, he decided that the occasion should be well worth writing about.

The first step was to appoint Darbishire chief Press Photographer, for Jennings was certain to be selected for the team. He was a promising player and had once had a trial for the 1st XI, but he was considered too young to hold a regular place among the thirteen-year-olds. Now, he had found his feet to some purpose as a keen and useful member of the 2nd XI. He was rather unwilling to allow Darbishire full control of the camera, but he was forced to admit that he could not possibly play centre half and take snapshots at the same time.

Darbishire was delighted. He had always wanted to be in charge of the camera and as he had no hope of being chosen for the 2nd XI, he was the obvious choice.

The next move was not so simple. School teams had never been known to take press-photographers with them, and there was the gravest doubt whether the Headmaster would grant the necessary permission. Better by far to apply for the job of linesman and hope that the duties would allow for a little amateur photography to be carried on during the course of the game.

To their surprise, the plan succeeded. Mr Carter, when approached, was quite willing to appoint Darbishire linesman, and Jennings spent the next few days coaching him for his two duties.

Darbishire was an apt learner. Soon he could take photographs without including his forefinger in the picture, and every night at bedtime he practised his linesmanship by charging up and down the dormitory waving his vest above his head, in place of a flag. Venables and Atkinson lent a hand by heading rolled-up socks over imaginary touchlines, so that he could give his decision about the throw-in. By the time Saturday arrived, he felt confident of coping with any problems of photography or flag-waving.

Mr Carter and Mr Wilkins took the team to Bracebridge School; they caught the bus to Dunhambury station and made the rest of the journey by train. The team was excited and eager, for not only were Bracebridge certain to give them a good game – they were also certain to give them a good tea afterwards.

When they reached their destination shortly after two o'clock, the Linbury team were taken upstairs to a dormitory to change: the linesman, having nothing to change, was shown into an empty classroom to await his colleagues.

It seemed odd to Darbishire to be in a school and yet form no part of it. It was not merely that the surroundings were different, for indeed the classroom was very similar to his own. There was the same smell of ink and chalk dust, the same over-full desks with lids which wouldn't quite shut: the lost rubbers hiding beneath the radiator and the badly-aimed balls of old blotting paper which had fallen short of the waste-paper basket, all seemed familiar. And yet, somehow, he did not feel quite at home. He sat down in a back row desk and read the history notes still chalked up on the blackboard.

Presently the door opened and a long crocodile of Bracebridge boys came winding in. They were about his own age, and in their grey jerseys and regulation school socks they might almost have been his Linbury colleagues. Only their faces were different.

The faces looked at Darbishire, mildly surprised to see a stranger in their midst.

"I've been told to wait here," he explained to a round-faced boy with large pink ears, who came and sat in the desk beside him.

"Why, what have you done wrong?" inquired the pink-eared one.

"Nothing, I'm the Linbury linesman and special press photographer."

"Oh! Well if I were you, I'd beat it before old Foxy Type gets his gun-sights on you."

"Who's Foxy Type?"

"Huh! You'll soon find out if you stick around these parts," came the cryptic answer.

By this time, the Bracebridge crocodile had occupied all the desks and overflowed onto the benches at the back of the room. There must have been about thirty of them, Darbishire reckoned. He felt suddenly aware that he was intruding; he would beat a retreat, as advised, and find his own way to the football pitch. He picked up his camera and his flag and rose to make his way out of the room.

"Sit down, that boy!" rasped a crisp, metallic voice; and looking up, he saw that the master's desk was occupied by a hatchet-faced man with thinning hair and bushy eyebrows.

This, presumably, was Foxy Type! His gaze was directed downwards at a book on his desk and he had only caught the movement of a grey jersey from the corner of his eye.

Darbishire felt the time had come to explain.

"Excuse me, sir…" he began; but he got no further for the master, still with averted gaze, called out: "Quiet, that boy! One more word from anyone, and I'll have you all back here this evening, as well."

"But, sir…"

"Right! The whole lot of you will come back after tea!" Darbishire sat down again, conscious of the hostile atmosphere. He would obviously have to secure his release more tactfully. He raised his hand.

"Put that hand down!" said the master, without raising his eyes to see whom the hand belonged to.

Outside on the football pitch, a whistle blew. Darbishire grew tense with anxiety; the match had started, and nobody had come to fetch him. Instead of running up and down with his flag at the ready, here he was, a prisoner in a detention class, guarded by this curiously named F Type, Esq. It was a little hard, he told himself, that he who spent so much time trying to avoid being kept in at his own school should run *slap-bang-whomp* into this packet of trouble as soon as he set foot in Bracebridge. A nice way to treat an invited guest! Why, he didn't even know what he was being detained for!

Minutes ticked by, and still Darbishire sat and seethed with baffled fury. He felt as out of place as a chess champion in a rugger scrum. Would no one come to his rescue? He nudged his pink-eared neighbour, but the boy merely shrugged helplessly. It was clear that they had a healthy respect for this Mr Type, or whatever his name was.

"Stop fidgeting in the back row," came from the master's desk. "You're all going to sit still in perfect silence until I… "

The words trailed away, as the bushy eyebrows narrowed in a frown and a pair of steely blue eyes were focused on the back row desk. Mr Fox, alias Foxy Type, had spotted what was amiss.

"We appear to have caught an unusual – ah – specimen in our net," he said, with rather less edge on his voice. "I don't recollect having seen that face about the premises before; the loss, of course, is mine. But tell me, dear boy, to what are we indebted for the honour of this most delightful visit?"

"Please, sir, I got in by mistake," said Darbishire.

"Tut-tut! Too bad, too bad! And very careless of you," mused Mr Fox with heavy humour. "It is a well-known fact here at Bracebridge that my detention classes, like the humble spider's web, are easy to enter but extremely difficult to leave. Are you sure you wouldn't prefer to stay and keep us company?"

"Quite sure, thank you, sir."

"Pity! However, we won't press you, as you seem anxious to be on your way. But don't hesitate to come and pay us a visit, any time you're passing. We'll keep a desk aired for you."

Darbishire scuttled from the room and didn't stop scuttling till he had found his way to the football pitch. Things were not going too well, he thought.

But worse was to follow before the day was over.

10

Destination Unknown

If only Darbishire had made his escape a little earlier, he could have taken a photograph of the winning goal, which was scored by Temple in the opening minutes of the game. But by the time the linesman had arrived panting at his action station, the play had settled down to a level struggle between two well-matched sides, and no more goals were scored.

It was a good, fast game; too fast for Darbishire to make much use of the camera, for when the play was near his touchline he was too busy with his linesmanship, and when the ball veered across the pitch the players were too far away to be photographed.

Jennings did not discover this till they were in the railway carriage on their return journey.

"Smashing game, wasn't it, Darbi!" he said. "Did you get a photo of the winning goal?"

The cameraman had to confess that the only photograph he could be sure of was a snap of Bromwich sucking a lemon at half-time.

"Well, you're a bright sort of character, I must say!" Jennings complained. "For all the help you've been, you might just as well have been back at school sitting in the classroom."

Hastily, Darbishire changed the subject. "Supersonic tea, they gave us, wasn't it? That shepherd's pie was the best garbage I've tasted for months. I had three refills."

In the corner seat, Mr Carter raised a pained eyebrow.

"You had *what*, Darbisbire?"

"Oh, sorry, sir. I mean I had three helpings of that delicious dish, sir."

A mumble of protest arose all round the carriage. "Coo, that's not fair. Darbishire wolfing three helpings. I only got one," complained Venables bitterly.

"Same here," grumbled Temple. "They told me they'd run out of shepherds by the time I'd got enough space for refuelling; and no wonder with old Darbishire belting into it like nobody's business."

"I don't think the linesmen deserve any tea at all," added Atkinson. "After all, anyone can prance up and down the touchline like a lobster in elastic-sided boots, and wag a flag till he's black in the face."

"Hear, hear!" said all the players who had had less than three helpings.

It was clear that linesmen as a class were unpopular, so Darbishire turned to admire the scenery through the open carriage window. But his critics would allow him no peace.

"There you go – bishing up all the regulations," bristled Atkinson. "There's a warning about people like you over the door. Can't you read?"

Darbishire glanced upwards. *It is Dangerous for Passengers to put their Heads out of the Window*, he read.

"I didn't put my heads out," he defended himself. "I've only got one head to put out. That notice is bats. It ought to say – *No Passenger must put his own head out*."

"Fair enough! That means we can put somebody else's head out," said Bromwich. "Whose shall we put?"

"Darbishire's, of course – he's only the linesman," was the unanimous verdict of the critics.

Jennings rallied to his friend's assistance. "It's jolly well not fair, all setting on one chap. The trouble is the railway people aren't very good at bashing out notices. What they should say is *All passengers must not put his, her or its head out, respectively*."

"You couldn't put your head out respectively," Atkinson objected. "What you mean is, *reflectively*. Because if you did, and another train came along with a supersonic *whoosh-doyng*, it wouldn't half give you something to reflect about."

Mr Carter groaned quietly. One of the disadvantages of being a schoolmaster, he maintained, was that one had to listen to idiotic nonsense for long periods. However, the train was approaching Dunhambury station by this time, so his ordeal would not last much longer.

"Start getting your cases down, and don't leave anything on the rack," he ordered. "Have you got your gloves, Jennings?"

"I think so, sir. Here's one in my pocket, and the other's about somewhere, sir."

"Where are your football boots, Venables?"

"In my case, sir. I wrapped them in my clean towel because they were a bit muddy, sir."

The train slowed and stopped, and Mr Carter led the way onto the platform, while from the next carriage stepped Mr Wilkins and the rest of the team.

They had no time to waste, for the bus back to Linbury was due to leave in less than two minutes; so Mr Carter hurried ahead to detain it at the bus stop, leaving his colleague to marshal the boys on the platform and bring them along as quickly as possible.

"Come along, you boys, come *along*," commanded Mr Wilkins in a voice which could be heard clearly above the explosive wheezings of a goods engine standing at an adjoining platform. "Get into line, Rumbelow, you silly little boy. This is no time to go loco-spotting."

He turned and marched rapidly towards the barrier, with the team trotting obediently at his heels.

Jennings and Darbishire hurried along at the tail of the procession, but after they had gone a few yards, Jennings suddenly stopped. He dropped his suitcase and started beating his raincoat pockets as though coping with an outbreak of fire.

"What's the matter?" asked Darbishire.

"It's my glove. I've lost it! I must have left it in the train."

"Oh, fish-hooks! Are you sure?"

"Yes. I've got this one in my pocket, look, but there's not a sausage of the other one anywhere. Let's beetle back to the carriage and see if we can find it. We'll soon catch the others up, if we run."

Hastily they retraced their steps along the platform, as Mr Wilkins and the rest of the team disappeared through the barrier and out of the station with never a backward glance.

It took the glove-hunters some seconds to find their compartment. "Here we are," cried Darbishire, tugging at a door. "This must be the one, because it's got that notice about not sticking heads out of windows."

"They *all* say that, you crumbling clodpoll! Ours was much farther down."

Very soon they identified their carriage by a toffee-paper sticking to the window. In they jumped and searched frantically on the racks and beneath the seats. They found a newspaper, a bag of peanut shells and an empty tea-cup, but there was no sign of a fleecy-lined glove.

"It must be somewhere. Look harder!" Jennings urged.

"I *am* looking harder. My eyes are popping like balloons, but it just isn't here. I think we'd better get out now. The train will be starting in a…"

It was at that moment that a porter slammed the door behind them and waved a "right away" signal down the platform. The engine which, until then had been mumbling "*jigger-jigger-jigger*," suddenly became silent and pulled smoothly away from the platform.

"Oh gosh, it *is* starting!" yelled Darbishire in wild alarm. He made a dive for the carriage door, but was thwarted by the raised window from reaching the handle on the outside.

Jennings had leapt, too, and for a few feverish seconds all was confusion as he pulled downwards on the strap while Darbishire pushed upwards to lift the window-frame in its socket. By the time they realised they were working against one another, it was too late. The window came down with a bang as the end of the platform streaked past their horror-struck faces.

"Oh, golly, whatever shall we do?" moaned Darbishire, while Jennings leaned out of the window uttering vain cries for help.

"It's no earthly good doing that, Jen. No one'll hear you. Besides, it's dangerous to put your head out: the notice says so."

Jennings withdrew his head from the danger zone. "I'll pull the communication cord," he cried in reckless despair. "That's not dangerous, at any rate."

"It jolly well *is!* Unless, of course, you happen to have twenty-four pounds, ninety-seven pence on you. Go ahead and pull it, if you have, because I've got the other three pence to make up the twenty-five pounds fine."

A moment's reflection showed that Darbishire's advice was sound; pulling communication cords would only lead to more trouble. But something would have to be done, for although the situation was desperate already, it would become even worse when Mr Wilkins discovered what had happened. To

117

miss the bus by accident was bad enough, but to catch the train by accident was nothing less than a catastrophe.

Now that the first shock was over, Jennings felt cold and empty inside, but he refused to allow his feelings to get the better of him. He must keep calm and plan out the next move.

"Don't worry, Darbi," he said with forced assurance. "We'll just have to stay where we are till we get to the next station, and then we'll walk back and hope we haven't been missed."

Darbishire flapped his fingers and hopped from foot to foot in agitation. "But how do we know the train's going to *stop* at the next station? It might be an express – next stop Land's End or John o' Groats, or somewhere."

"It couldn't be both – not unless it went different ways at the same time," Jennings pointed out. "The real trouble is that Mr Carter's got our tickets, so it may be a bit tricky getting off the platform."

"Oh, fish-hooks! I hadn't thought of that. Why do these frantic hoo-hahs always have to pick on us to happen to? My father says that…"

"Never mind what your father says! And stop jigging about like a cow on an escalator – you're giving me the fidgets. We'll manage all right."

Darbishire slumped into a corner seat and watched the rolling downland speeding past the carriage window. In his mind he compiled a gloomy catalogue of their troubles: (*a*) Prosecution by railway company for travelling without ticket; (*b*) Persecution by Mr Wilkins for disobeying orders and being absent without leave; (*c*) Listed at local police station as Missing Persons with no visible means of support. And all because that prize bazooka, Jennings, had achieved new heights of clodpollery by losing his… Darbishire abandoned his catalogue and sat bolt upright, his eyes staring in amazement.

"I say, Jennings: there's your other glove, look – on your hand!"

Jennings shook his head. "No, it isn't. This is the one I *haven't* lost."

"But it can't be. You said you'd got the other one in your pocket."

Jennings' hand shot up to his mouth in guilty realisation. Then he felt in his pocket and produced the missing glove.

"Oh, heavens! Yes, you're right, Darbi. I was so busy searching my pockets for the second one I didn't spot I'd got it on all the time. What a decent bit of luck you noticed it!"

Darbishire thumped the carriage cushions with exasperation. "Luck! Gosh, I like the cheek of that! You land us *slap-bang-wallop* into the most supersonic bish since the Battle of Hastings and then sit there calmly talking about decent chunks of luck! Dash it all, Jen, here we are tearing off towards Land's End or somewhere at a hundred miles an hour, and before we know where we are, we'll find ourselves – goodness knows where!"

"No, it's *after* we know where we are that we'll find out where we've got to, because…"

Just then the train slowed down and both boys swivelled round to the window. A platform came into view, then a station sign-board marked Pottlewhistle Halt.

There was no doubt about it – they were stopping, and Jennings felt his spirits rising with renewed hope.

"Well, it's not Land's End, anyway, or we'd be able to see the Scilly Isles," he observed with an attempt at heartiness.

"Don't talk to me about the Scilly Isles. I *could* make a frightfully witty remark about a silly something else I can see, but I don't think this is the moment for jokes, somehow. My father says there's a time and place for everything."

119

"He's right for once, too," Jennings replied, as the train stopped and he opened the carriage door. "This is the time and place for getting out of the train."

It was a very small station. From the wooden shanty which served as booking-office and waiting-room an elderly porter came out and shouted what sounded like "*Poliwillall!... Pollwillall!*"

But nobody else left the train in spite of this invitation, and Jennings seized Darbishire's arm and drew him into the shelter afforded by a stack of milk churns. The porter was looking towards the front of the train and had not noticed them, but with no other passengers to cover their retreat, caution was necessary.

They crouched behind the milk churns hardly daring to breathe, and a moment later they heard the scrunch of heavy boots as the porter marched flat-footedly down the platform to the guard's van.

There was a thud as a sack of fertilizer was dropped onto the platform, and an even louder one as a crate of eggs was heaved into the van. Then the train moved on, the footsteps approached the milk churns, passed by and died away as the porter lumbered back into the booking-office.

Jennings heaved a sigh of relief. "Phew! He never spotted us, thank goodness! Come on, we'd better beat it while the coast's clear. It'll be dark in two shakes of a lamb's tail."

Behind them a low wooden fence ran the length of the platform, and the boys had no difficulty in climbing over and onto the country lane beyond. Jennings was beginning to enjoy himself. It was, he felt, something of an adventure.

Not so, Darbishire. The camera slung round his neck might have been a millstone and his linesman's flag hung limp and drooping as though in surrender. In addition to his other troubles his conscience had started to worry him about travelling the extra distance without a ticket: he made a mental note to send the railway company ten pence in stamps at the earliest opportunity.

"I've had enough of this," he complained, peering shortsightedly into the gathering gloom. "Strikes me it's more dangerous than sticking your head out of the window. Still, it's your fault we're here, so you'd better start leading the way back."

It was a reasonable suggestion: the only snag about it was that Jennings had not the slightest idea which way to go, and could see no signpost to guide him.

Pottlewhistle Halt was a station which seemed to have been built with no clear purpose in mind, for it was situated in open country, some distance from the nearest village. No bus route served it, few passengers used it, and only the slowest of trains ever stopped there. It did, however, possess an old-world charm, and the view from the platform was delightful.

The South Downs lay on either side and a country lane wound its way past the station, up the hill, and through a little wood. After that it climbed the steep slope of the Downs and branched out into a network of footpaths.

"I vote we follow this lane. We're bound to strike the Linbury road after a few miles," Jennings decided.

"A few miles – phew! You seem to forget I've been hoofing up and down the touchline all afternoon, wagging my flag. I think we ought to ask someone if it's the right way first."

"How can we? There's no one about to ask."

"Ask the old porter – he's about."

Jennings shook his head. "Don't be such a prehistoric remains, Darbi! We've got to keep out of his way in case he finds out about the tickets. Why, it'd be a wizard sight more dangerous asking him than putting your head out of the window."

It was growing dark as they set off up the hill and there was a peaceful stillness in the evening air which did much to comfort Darbishire's anxiety.

"It's supersonic scenery round these parts; rather like Gray's *Elegy* that Mr Carter was reading to us last week," he observed. "I can just imagine the lowing herd winding slowly o'er the lea and the ploughman homeward plodding his weary way; can't you?"

"Better wait till we've actually plodded home before you start nattering about weary ways," Jennings advised. "If we don't get weaving a bit faster than this the curfew will have tolled the knell of parting day before you can say 'Fossilised fish-hooks.'"

11

The Search Party

As the five o'clock bus from Dunhambury left the town and sped along the Linbury road, Mr Carter turned to his colleague in the seat behind him.

"It's as well I ran ahead and stopped the bus. There isn't another one for two hours," he said.

Mr Wilkins nodded. He was still breathing heavily from the exertion of shepherding his flock along the road to the bus stop at a brisk eight miles an hour. Now, at last, he could relax.

"I suppose you counted to make sure that all the team were with you?" Mr Carter asked.

"Well, actually, no, I didn't," Mr Wilkins admitted. "What with you holding the bus back for us, and the conductor waving to us to get a move on, I didn't have time. But you needn't worry, Carter; they're all here, right enough. I'll count them now, if it'll make you feel any happier."

The bright red caps of Linbury Court School were easily distinguishable in the crowded vehicle, and Mr Wilkins could see them all from where he sat – Venables and Atkinson in the front seats, with Temple and Bromwich just behind: across the gangway he noted Rumbelow, Martin-Jones, Binns and Nuttall, and in the back row were Parslow and Thompson.

"That's queer! I can only see ten," muttered Mr Wilkins. "There must be one I haven't counted."

"There should be *two* more," corrected Mr Carter. "Eleven in the team, plus a linesman makes… Linesman! Yes, of course; where are Jennings and Darbishire?"

Mr Wilkins looked baffled for a moment. Then he said: "They *must* be on the bus, somewhere. Perhaps they've gone upstairs."

"Upstairs!" Mr Carter's voice rose in shocked surprise. "This, Wilkins, is a *single-decker* bus!"

"Eh, what's that! I… I… Corwumph! Good heavens, so it is. I never noticed!"

"Well, really, Wilkins! You were responsible for seeing everyone off the platform. Surely I can leave a simple job like that to…"

"All right, all right, all *right!*" Mr Wilkins was inclined to grow excitable at times of crisis. He leapt to his feet for a rapid recount, calling loudly: "Hands up, everybody! Put your hands up; I want to see who's here."

The Linbury boys obeyed, and a middle-aged lady with a shopping basket shot both hands towards the ceiling, under the impression that an armed hold-up was in progress.

"Quickly, now. Hands up all the boys who aren't here – er, I mean, has anyone seen Jennings and Darbishire?"

Again he counted, but the total remained obstinately at ten.

"Are you sure they're not here, sir?" queried Thompson.

"Of course I'm sure, you silly little boy. They wouldn't have put their hands up if they were; or rather, they would have put them up if they…oh, be quiet!" Mr Wilkins was feeling rather confused. Action, prompt and immediate, was called for, and he pushed his way along to the door at the back. "I say, conductor, stop the bus! You're going the wrong way – I mean, I want to get off!"

By now, the team was agog with excitement and the other passengers were seething with curiosity.

"Just like old Jennings to go and make a bish of things!"

"Perhaps they were in a hurry, so they've run on ahead."

The bus buzzed with wild speculation, and the lady with the shopping basket crouched low in her seat, expecting any second to hear the sharp crack of revolver shots. She had spent the afternoon watching a gangster film at the Dunhambury cinema, and the memory was still vivid.

It was Mr Carter who restored order and persuaded his colleague to return to his seat. He pointed out that no useful purpose would be served by alighting on a deserted country road two miles from the town. By the time they had walked back, it would be dark and they would probably miss the boys in the maze of streets near the station. Far better, he reasoned, to return to school first and telephone the station to see if they were still there.

"They may even have got back on the train to retrieve their belongings and been carried on to the next stop," he pointed out with brilliant guesswork.

"And where's the next stop – Brighton?" snorted Mr Wilkins.

"Oh, no. It's only a local train. The next station is a little place called Pottlewhistle Halt."

"I'll *Pottlewhistle Halt* them if they have! I tell you, Carter, when I get hold of Jennings and Darbishire I'll… I'll…well, they'd better look out!"

"Quite. But if *you'd* looked out at the bus stop it would have saved a lot of trouble," Mr Carter reminded him.

Soon the bus drew up at the school gates, and when the remaining five-sixths of the team had been hustled indoors, the two masters made for the telephone in Mr Carter's study and put through a call to Dunhambury station. Unfortunately, no one there could throw any light on the whereabouts of the two boys and the senior master wore a worried frown as he replaced the receiver.

"I'll go along and tell the Head at once," he said. At the door, he turned and added: "If you want to be useful, Wilkins, you can phone the next station down the line and see if they got off there."

"Yes, of course; I'll do it right away." And Mr Wilkins strode over to the telephone as the door closed behind his colleague.

The next station down the line! That would be... Mr Wilkins paused in the act of picking up the receiver. What *was* the name that Carter had mentioned in the bus? Whistlepottle Halt?... Pottlewhistle Halt?... Or was it Haltpottle Whistle? Mr Wilkins could not be sure.

"It's either Whistlehalt Pottle or Pottlehalt Whistle," he muttered to himself as he sat with the receiver to his ear, waiting for *Enquiries* to come to his aid.

When it did, he said: "Oh, hullo, *Enquiries!* Can you put me through to a station called Whistlepott Hortle, please?... What's that? There's no such place? Well, try Haltpottle Whistle, then."

The operator regretted that she couldn't find that place either, but after Mr Wilkins had suggested Haltwhistle Pottle and Pittlewhostle Halt, she said she thought she knew where the caller meant.

"Oh, good – that's more than *I* do," said the caller thankfully; and a few moments later the voice of the elderly porter sounded on the line.

"Hullo, are you Whistlehalt Pott? I want to speak to the stationmaster, please," said Mr Wilkins.

A burring Sussex accent replied that the stationmaster had gone home to his tea.

"Well, never mind, you'll do just as well if you're the Whistlehalt Pott porter. Can you tell me whether the last train from Dunhambury halted at Pottlewhistle Stop? Er, stopped at Pottlewhistle Halt?... Oh, good. Well, did you notice if two boys in school caps alighted at the station?"

The voice replied that there wasn't much at Poliwillall for *anyone* to feel pleased about.

"No, no, no. I said *a*lighted, not *de*lighted. I asked you whether they got off."

There was a pause at the other end of the line, and then the voice declared that it was a funny thing that he should be asked that question: for bless his soul if he hadn't seen two boys walking away from the station towards Cowpatch Wood just after the train had left. He had thought to himself that such a thing was queer – distinctly queer, seeing as how he hadn't seen them get off the train – but there it was!

"Thank you very much. Goodbye!" Mr Wilkins replaced the receiver, and heaved a sigh of relief.

Now, at least, they knew roughly where the boys had got to. All that was needed was for some responsible person to walk over the Downs towards Pottle-whatever-it-was, and meet them.

He hurried from the room and along to the Headmaster's study where he found Mr Pemberton-Oakes frowning over Mr Carter's news.

"But this is ridiculous, Carter," the Headmaster was saying. "Surely we can win a football match without losing part of the team in the process! I shall telephone the police station immediately."

"It's all right – I've found them," Mr Wilkins burst out. "Or, rather, I know where they are."

"Oh, good! You got through to Pottlewhistle Halt then?" asked Mr Carter.

"So that's what it's called, is it! You might have told me," replied his colleague. "Yes, I've been through, and the Pottleport Halt whistler – er, the Whistlehalt Pott porter – er – the man in charge of the station saw them making for some woods."

The Headmaster continued to frown thoughtfully. It was quite dark now and the boys might easily lose their way – if, indeed, they ever knew it in the first place – among the criss-crossing footpaths which led over the Downs to Linbury. Now, what would be the best course to pursue, he wondered?... Ah! He had it! A search-party of some half-dozen or more persons equipped with torches and whistles would be the best way of contacting the missing boys in the darkness.

The rest of the school were having tea, and time would be lost in selecting and briefing suitable boys for their tasks; but the 2nd XI, still in their outdoor shoes and raincoats, could set off at once. They were the obvious choice, for they had had their tea at Bracebridge and already knew the purpose of the search.

Five minutes later, the ten remaining members of the team were standing in a group on the quad, listening to their instructions.

"We're going over the Downs towards Pottlewhistle," Mr Carter told them. "Jennings and Darbishire are bound to be approaching from that direction, so we'll all keep together until you're given the order to spread out and search. Then you'll keep in touch by listening for whistle signals. Three long blasts will mean that you're to report back to Mr Wilkins or to me at once. Now, have you all got torches?"

"I told them to go and collect them," said Mr Wilkins. "We shall need them too, because... Oh, I say, Carter, I haven't got one myself! In the heat of the moment I quite forgot to go and fetch it."

Mr Carter sighed. He felt that the search-party would get on much better if only Mr Wilkins would agree to stay at home; for with his colleague playing a major part in the expedition, there was always the chance that they would lose the rest of the team instead of finding the two who were missing.

But Mr Carter didn't say so. Instead, he asked: "Has any boy got a torch to lend Mr Wilkins?"

"Yes, I have, sir. Here you are, sir: you can have this one," said Temple generously.

"Thank you," said Mr Wilkins. "Are you sure you won't need it yourself?"

"Oh, no, sir, that's all right. It's no good to me, sir – it hasn't got a battery."

"I... I... *Corwumph!* But, you silly little boy, what's the good of..."

"I think we'd better be going," said Mr Carter hastily. "Just stand still while I count you all."

He switched on his torch and checked carefully; ten boys, plus two masters. Satisfied, he gave the order. "Right: lead on down the drive, Venables!"

The search-party was on its way!

The network of lanes and footpaths between Pottlewhistle and Linbury offers a choice of picturesque walks on fine summer afternoons. On dark November evenings, however, they lose much of their charm, and by the time Jennings and Darbishire had covered three miles they were beginning to tire of the Sussex countryside.

If only they had followed the road, they might – with luck – have found their way back to school unaided; but unfortunately Jennings trusted to his sense of direction to guide them safely through what he hoped was a short-cut.

It wasn't; and very soon they had to admit that they were hopelessly lost. For twenty minutes they followed a footpath which led them to the summit of a grassy hill. Then, for no apparent reason, the path stopped short like an escalator disappearing below ground level.

"Oh, fish-hooks, this is feeble!" lamented Darbishire. "We must have walked about a thousand miles, and I'm so hungry I'm beginning to rattle. What couldn't I do with a few more re-fills of that shepherd's pie!"

"If only we could be sure we were going the right way," said Jennings in a worried voice. "We may be walking round and round in circles like chaps in a fog."

"Or in the desert," Darbishire added gloomily. "They walk for miles through never-ending sand and then, when they're just about dead from hunger, they see supersonic oasis-*es* with masses of stuff to eat like boxes of dried dates and palm trees."

"If I saw a mirage I'd rather it was bulging with shepherd's pie."

"M'yes, but you wouldn't be able to eat it, because you can only see mirages properly when they aren't there," Darbishire explained. "Or rather, when they *are* there, you can't see them quite plainly, if you see what I mean. That's why they call them mirages, and my father says..."

"Oh, don't talk such aerated eyewash, Darbi," said Jennings, coming to a halt. "The only thing I can see quite plainly is that it's too dark to see anything at all. Why, I can hardly see my hand in front of my face."

Darbishire sank down on the damp grass for a rest. "I shouldn't strain your eyes trying to. It's only..."

"Oh, goodness!" Jennings abandoned his hand-raising experiment and turned towards his reclining friend in dismay. "I say, Darbi – what do you think?"

"I don't know. Whatever I think it's bound to be wrong – it always is," came in complaining tones from ground level. "Go on, you tell me what I think if you're so clever."

"I've lost my glove again!"

"You can't have lost it *again*, because you never really lost it properly the first time. I expect you've got it on. Have a look and see."

Curtly Jennings pointed out that if it was too dark to see his hand in front of his face, there was little chance of seeing his glove there, either. He turned back along the way they had come and followed the path down the hill for a few yards. He knew his glove couldn't be far away for he remembered twirling both of them round and round like propellers, less than five minutes before.

Wearily, Darbishire rose to his feet and followed his friend down the path. He was cold and hungry and very unhappy; but as he was lost anyway, it mattered little to him whether they went forward or retraced their steps.

For a hundred yards they wended their way, feeling with their feet and stopping now and again to investigate some black shape which turned out, on closer inspection, to be a mole-hill or a tussock of grass.

"I'm just about fed up to the eardrums with all this mooching about," Darbishire complained. "I wish there was someone about we could ask. If only there was a ploughman homeward plodding his weary way, or even a double-decker bus winding slowly o'er the lea that we could catch."

"You've got a hope!" Jennings retorted. "We're more likely to catch frostbite from being marooned all night with only one glove. I bet there isn't another person about for miles."

It was then that they heard the whistle – three long, low blasts sounding distantly from the bottom of the hill. Jennings gripped his friend's arm and his voice throbbed with excitement.

"I say, Darbi, did you hear a whistle just then?"

"That wasn't a whistle: that was a moping owl," Darbishire decided.

"But there were three of them!"

"All right then, three moping owls; or the same owl moping three times. Besides, owls don't whistle; they go *tu-whit tu-whoo* and to the moon complain, of such as wandering near…"

"Oh, shut up! I wish you'd leave Gray's *Elegy* out of this. Listen, there it is again!"

There was no doubt about it. The blasts were nearer now, and with a sudden start of joy, Jennings recognised them. "Oh wacko! It's Mr Carter's referee whistle."

Darbishire was sceptical. "You're bats! How could it be? You must be hearing things."

"Of course I'm hearing things. I just heard Mr Carter's whistle."

"No, I mean you're hearing things that aren't there. It's probably a mirage, only as it's too dark to see, it's affecting your ears instead of your eyes."

But a few moments later the "mirage" grew more distinct and the whistles were followed by distant shouts and the flashing of torches. Then the shouts sounded closer, and the boys recognised Venables' high-pitched voice and heard Atkinson call in reply. Shortly after that a beam of torchlight fell upon Temple and Martin-Jones coming up the grass slope at right-angles to the footpath. Another torch flashed away to the left, and Mr Wilkins' stentorian bellow could be heard telling Bromwich to look where he was walking.

"The whole team's there," Jennings gasped in surprise. "Fancy meeting them wandering about miles from anywhere. They seem to be looking for something too. I wonder what on earth it can be!"

Oddly enough, it never occurred to either Jennings or Darbishire that they might be the object of the search. To them, the most likely explanation was that the team had missed the bus at Dunhambury and were walking back to school over the Downs. Perhaps they, too, had tried to take a short-cut with unfortunate results.

"Wacko! We're rescued! Let's beetle down the hill in top gear and join them," cried Darbishire.

But Jennings advised caution. It was just possible, he reasoned, that in the scurry of missing the bus and hampered by the approach of darkness, no one had noticed their absence. After all, who could tell, without a careful check, whether there were ten boys or twelve in the party? If, then, he and Darbishire announced their return to the fold with joyful wacko's and hearty back-slappings, Mr Wilkins would realise that they had not been amongst those present during the past hour. He would probe into the matter; unpleasant facts about accidental train rides would emerge and a whole chapter of misfortunes would come to light which would be better forgotten.

"Yes, there's something in that," Darbishire agreed. "What had we better do, then?"

"We'll just join up with them quietly, one at a time, and not say much, for a kick-off. They won't notice in the dark; and when they've found the way, we'll all get back to school without anyone knowing we haven't been with them all the time. Go on, you hoof off and join them, and I'll follow in a minute."

Darbishire set off down the path, taking care to keep out of the beams of the torches sweeping over the hillside. Jennings watched until his friend was swallowed up in the darkness: then he strolled slowly after him.

12

The Shades of Night

Halfway up the hill, Mr Wilkins paused to rally his forces.

"Keep together, you boys. Don't straggle, or you'll get lost. And if anyone thinks he hears a... Be quiet, Venables, when I'm talking!"

"I was being quiet, sir."

"Well, don't be quiet so loudly! It's difficult enough to keep track of you in the dark without... Now, where's Mr Carter got to?"

"He's still over by that barn, sir. I heard his whistle a moment ago," said a voice in the darkness.

"Good! I'll give an answering whistle so he can join us, and then we'll press on." Mr Wilkins searched through his pockets in vain. "Tut-tut-tut! I seem to have left my whistle behind at school."

"I can lend you one, sir," said another disembodied voice. "It isn't much of a thing, though. I got it out of a cracker last Christmas, sir."

"Never mind where you got it, so long as it works." Mr Wilkins groped in the gloom and found himself holding a thin wooden reed, barely an inch long.

In the distance, three long, low blasts boomed out like a lightship's siren as Mr Carter sought to make contact with the main party. Immediately, Mr Wilkins put the toy whistle to his lips and blew with all the strength of a north-easterly gale. A thin, high-pitched *pheep-pheep*, like the chirrup of a newly-hatched chick, was audible at a distance of three yards, and the boys around the whistler collapsed with laughter.

"Oh, sir! What a feeble whistle, sir!"

"Golly, sir! Is that your famous jet-propelled, short wave radar transmitter, sir?"

"I... I... *Corwumph!* Be quiet and listen to me. When we get to the top of this hill, half of you will go with Mr Carter towards Haltpottle and the rest will come with me towards... Who's that boy straying about? I said no one was to go wandering off."

"I think it's Atkinson, sir," guessed Temple: though, in point of fact, it was Darbishire making a roundabout approach.

"No, it's not me; I'm here, sir," Atkinson's voice piped up from the outer darkness.

Mr Wilkins strained his eyes trying to identify the shapes milling around him. "I can't see who's here and who isn't. Stand still, everybody – I'm going to count you."

He marched round the little group, prodding each boy in the chest and calling his number aloud. A note of bewilderment crept into his voice as he reached the end of his census. "...eight, nine, ten, *eleven!*"

Eleven! It couldn't possibly be eleven: they had had only ten to start with!

Mr Carter arrived at that moment. He was followed at a discreet distance by Jennings, who passed unseen into the midst of the group, as Mr Wilkins turned to his colleague in despair.

"This is hopeless, Carter! I'm trying to count these boys and they keep moving about in the dark."

"Is anyone missing – apart from the two we're looking for?"

"I don't think so. The last time I counted it came to one more than it should have done." The master's voice sounded strained as he started his check all over again. "One, two, three, four, five...tut-tut, I don't know whether I've counted that boy over there. Is it you Bromwich?"

"I don't know, sir; I can't see."

"You don't *have* to see, Bromo. You know if it's you, don't you?" said Venables.

"Oh yes, this is me all right, but I don't know whether I've been counted," Bromwich explained.

The note of strain in Mr Wilkins' voice grew more marked as he grappled with his counting.

"...six, seven, eight, nine, ten, eleven, *TWELVE!*"

The last word was uttered in a strangled squeak, as though the speaker's vocal cords were strung to the tension of a violin's E string.

Twelve! The thing was fantastic! Somebody must have moved twice; or perhaps two people had moved once; perhaps... Mr Wilkins gave it up. At any rate, their numbers were not short, so now they could press on with the business in hand.

The party moved slowly up the hill, straining their eyes and ears for any sign of the missing boys. But they did not look behind them or they might have observed that the objects of their search had attached themselves to the fringe of the group. As they wandered on, Jennings peered about as keenly as the official searchers, for he was still hoping to find his fleecy-lined glove.

At the top of the hill they all stopped to pick up their bearings and the two masters held a short conference.

"This seems to be the end of the path, Carter," said Mr Wilkins doubtfully. "Now I wonder what lies over there to the north?"

137

"I think it's the way back to Pottlewhistle Halt, sir," said Jennings helpfully.

"Don't interrupt, boy, when I'm talking to Mr Carter. I've had enough of Whistlehalt Pott for one evening, and besides..."

Mr Wilkins stopped abruptly. The voice from the darkness had had a familiar ring. For a moment he could have sworn it was... But how could it be? "Which boy spoke just then?" he demanded loudly.

"I did, sir," replied seven boys who were enjoying a lively discussion about how far cats could see in the dark.

"No, no, no – not you people! Somebody else; I was almost sure..." He turned again to his colleague. "I say, Carter, I'm hearing things. Somebody spoke just then, and it sounded like Jennings."

"That's just wishful thinking, I'm afraid."

"Yes, I suppose it must have been. This business is getting me down. I tell you, Carter. I'll be thankful when this wild-goose chase is over. I wouldn't be surprised if those two silly little boys have turned up at school by this time, and here we are traipsing about all over the countryside, and..."

A loud shout came from a patch of shadow a few yards to the right.

"Ooh, sir! Quick, sir! Come over here, sir – I've found something."

"Who's that?"

"It's me, sir – Temple. I've just found a glove by this rabbit hole, sir."

Instantly, torches clicked on and beams of light were focused on the speaker. Temple was kneeling on the turf a few paces down the hill, and in his hand was a fleecy-lined glove. He screwed up his eyes as he held the name tab up towards the torchlight.

"*J C T Jennings*. I've found Jennings' glove," he shouted in triumph.

"Wacko!" cried the owner, but his exclamation was lost in the stampede to investigate the find at close quarters.

The discovery put new heart into the searchers. Here was a clue which proved that they were on the right track after all. Why, with any luck the absentees might even be within earshot, and Mr Wilkins lost no time in giving his instructions.

"We'll all shout together at the top of our voices," he commanded. "Take a deep breath, everyone, Now! One, two, three…"

"*JEN-NINGS!*" A vast wave of sound rolled over the quiet downland, scaring the wild creatures of the night and setting the farm dogs barking in the valley below. Faintly, the echo returned from the surrounding hills… "*JEN-NINGS!*"

"Yes, sir?" said Jennings briskly.

He was standing just behind Mr Wilkins, and he had to sidestep smartly as the master recoiled from the shock and swung round like a rotating gun-turret.

"I… I… I… *Corwumph!* Who spoke then? Who said 'Yes, sir'?"

"Me, sir – Jennings. I thought I heard you calling me. Sir."

"But…but…you're standing right here in the middle of us!"

"Yes, sir. I wondered why you were shouting so loudly, sir."

It was perhaps as well that Mr Wilkins' features were obscured by the shades of night, and that the emotions searing through him were not visible to the naked eye. His jaw dropped through thirty degrees and his lips moved as though he would speak. But, for the moment, the fount of speech was dry.

The rest of the party were equally surprised by Jennings' unexpected appearance. They surged round him, voicing exclamations of disbelief.

"I say, it's not *really* you, is it, Jen?"

"Of course it's me. And old Darbi's about somewhere, too. We've been here some time."

"Why didn't you say so before?"

"Well, nobody asked me before."

"If you want to know what *I* think, you've no business to be here at all. You're supposed to be lost," grumbled Martin-Jones. He felt, somehow, that he was being cheated.

Mr Carter rescued Jennings and Darbishire from the jostling crowd around them. He listened to a brief outline of their misfortunes, and wisely decided to leave the details until they had returned to school.

"Well, I'm glad we've found you at last," he said. "We've been searching high and low."

"Yes, sir; so have I," Jennings answered.

"*You've* been searching? Whatever for?"

"For my glove, sir. Wasn't it a good job Temple found it! Matron would have been awfully fed up if I'd gone back without it, sir."

"*Doh!*" An anguished gasp of exasperation rang out loud and clear as Mr Wilkins found his voice again. "I... I... Really, Carter, it's too much! Anyone would think we'd got nothing better to do all night than grope our way round the rural parish of Whistlepottle like a pack of moles."

"Never mind, Wilkins; we can start making for home now."

"Yes, yes, yes, I know, but the whole thing's too ridiculous, Carter! Here we have been traipsing round looking for two wretched little boys, who have been traipsing round with us looking for a wretched little glove!"

As they descended the hill, Darbishire sought out Jennings and fell into step beside him.

"I say, did you hear what Mr Wilkins said just then, Jennings?" he asked. "If we're still somewhere near

Pottlewhistle we must have been walking round in circles like chaps in a mirage."

"Huh! A mirage is nothing to get excited about," his friend answered as he pulled on his newly-found glove. "Just look at Old Wilkie – *he's* walking round in circles like a chap in a trance!"

It was late when the search-party reached Linbury Court and later still before the boys had finished their supper. But despite the lateness of the hour, Jennings and Darbishire were summoned to the Headmaster's study before they were allowed to go upstairs to their dormitory.

They spent an uncomfortable twenty minutes listening to Mr Pemberton-Oakes' reproving words, and wondering what action he was going to take when he came to the end of them. Many of his observations they had heard before, and it was no news to them that he was "somewhat at a loss to understand" their motives, or that he "asked himself why they should fail to observe the rules of civilised behaviour."

But behind the Headmaster's ponderous words was a feeling of relief that the boys had come to no harm. He was a fair-minded man and he realised that the escapade was due more to muddle-headed reasoning than to disobedience. However, as the culprits had caused a great deal of trouble, neither of them would be allowed to accompany a school team to an "away" match for the rest of the term.

Jennings and Darbishire went upstairs to their dormitory in a subdued frame of mind.

"Talk about mouldy luck!" Jennings complained. "It's not so bad for you because you're not in the team, but there are at least four more 'away' matches I shall have to miss; and some of those schools dish out a supersonic tea after the game."

"Never mind, you'll be able to spend more time on our mag," Darbishire consoled him. "We ought to be getting the next number out pretty soon, now."

"With a nice front-page picture of the winning goal in the Bracebridge match, I suppose!"

Jennings wasn't going to let his assistant forget his shortcomings as a press-photographer. "Honestly, Darbi, you're about as handy with a camera as a cart-horse on stilts. You turn up when the game's half over and load yourself up with three refills of shepherd's pie before anyone else can even get their forks on the job. If you want to know what *I* think, you've bished up the whole day. I should never have left my glove in the train if I hadn't been worrying myself bald-headed about what you were going to get up to next."

"But you *didn't* leave it in the train. And besides..." Darbishire stopped. The criticism was grossly unfair, but perhaps it might be better not to argue about the photographs of the Bracebridge match while the little matter of shepherd's pie still rankled in the minds of the team. They would have to think of something else for the front page – the story of their accidental train ride, for instance: that should make good reading!

In his mind's eye he pictured the banner headlines: *Jennings and Darbishire Discover Search Party...* And underneath, in smaller type: *Search Party Discover Fleecy-Lined Glove.*

The story sounded so promising that he reached for his diary and began writing a rough draft as he sat up in bed.

An enthusiastic gathering took place near Pottlewhistle Halt last Saturday evening, when the mysterious disappearance of a missing glove led to an interesting episode, he wrote. *Asked by our Special Correspondent to comment on the proceedings, Mr L P Wilkins, the well-known schoolmaster, said...*

But at that moment, Mr Carter put out the dormitory light and the observations of Mr L P Wilkins were, fortunately, lost in the darkness.

In the next bed, Jennings, too, was pondering on the comments of the "well-known schoolmaster." Mr Wilkins, it seemed, had taken the events of the evening badly. On the way home he had announced firmly that never again would he make a journey by land, sea or air, if either Jennings or Darbishire were included in the party.

This was quite the wrong attitude, Jennings thought. A little more friendly give and take was needed, and less of this gunning for innocent victims like trigger-happy outlaws of the middle west. However, masters always had everything their own way, so if Mr Wilkins felt aggrieved, Jennings felt it was up to him to put matters right. He would show his willingness by working his hardest in class, and by laughing the loudest whenever Mr Wilkins made a joke. He would make cheerful conversation and be on the spot to open doors: he would... Yes, why not? A vague thought which had been ambling aimlessly round his mind for some days now leapt to attention and proclaimed itself a Bright Idea.

Jennings leaned out of bed and reached towards Darbishire. His fingers made contact with a lock of curly hair: he tugged gently.

"Oh, shut up! I was just going off to sleep," came in muffled tones from the next bed.

"Yes, but listen: I've got a massive wheeze. You know we were wondering what we could put in the *Form Three Times* instead of a competition?"

"A fine time to wake me up with wheezes!"

"Ah, but this is urgent. I've just thought how would it be if I wrote some life-stories of famous characters like, say, for instance, Julius Caesar and Oliver Cromwell and all those bods?"

"Sounds a bit feeble to me."

"Yes, but that's not all. Old Wilkie's got his gun-sights on us, so I thought it might put him in a decent mood."

"Why should *he* want to read about Oliver Cromwell?"

Jennings clicked his tongue impatiently. "No, you clodpoll! We'd include Old Wilkie in our *Famous Lives*, and perhaps some of the other masters too."

"We'd better call them *in*famous lives then and bung in a few chronic characters like Nero and Macbeth to keep him company," mumbled Darbishire sleepily.

"Oh, no; we've got to be really decent to Wilkie for a bit," Jennings decided as he smoothed his pillow. "After all, we owe him something for all the trouble he went to tonight."

13

The Initial Difficulty

Unfortunately, the *let's-be-decent-to-Wilkie* campaign was not an immediate success. During the next few days Jennings and Darbishire performed many acts of kindness designed to brighten Mr Wilkins' life and smooth his troubled path.

They almost mended his fountain pen for him after Jennings had accidentally knocked it off the desk; they woke him from an after-lunch snooze to ask whether he would care to see a water-colour of a strato-cruiser which Darbishire had just painted; and they helped him to blow up the footballs – until, by some mischance, Jennings punctured a new bladder with the football lacer.

But their efforts to lend a helping hand struck no answering chord in Mr Wilkins' heart.

"It's almost as though he doesn't *want* to be done good to," Jennings observed, as they waited for the master to arrive for an algebra lesson, a week after the campaign had started.

"Perhaps he'll be a bit more friendly when he sees what a decent write-up we give him in our magazine," Darbishire replied. "How are you getting on with those famous life-stories, by the way?"

"Fairly well. I've done Julius Caesar, but there wasn't much to say about Oliver Cromwell, so I'm going to do one of Mr

Carter to help fill up the space. Mr Wilkins is the most awkward one, though: I can't find out how old he is or what his initials stand for, or anything. It's jolly difficult writing a chap's biography when his past is just a closed book."

They spoke in whispers, as though fearful of disturbing the scholarly atmosphere which the Headmaster had told them should prevail before the start of a lesson: but though the room was quiet, the atmosphere was not so scholarly as it might have been

Temple was twanging soft notes on a guitar made from elastic bands stretched across his pencil box; Atkinson was dredging pellets of blotting paper from his inkwell and using them to block up the cracks between the floorboards. Bromwich was making a watch chain with paper clips and Venables was contorting his facial muscles in an effort to look like a slant-eyed oriental. It was, in short, an ordinary class waiting for the lesson to begin.

Nor had they long to wait. Heavy footsteps sounded in the corridor, the door swung back, shivering on its hinges, and Mr Wilkins made his usual brisk entrance.

"Good morning, sir," said Form Three politely.

" 'Morning. I'm going to show you a new sort of sum this lesson, so sit up straight and keep your wits about you."

Form Three sat up, but the keeping of wits about them was a different matter, for Mr Wilkins' explanation of the new sums was not easy to follow. There was, for example, the problem of the man who walked at the odd speed of x miles an hour for the unusual time of y hours.

Jennings was unwilling to believe that such a thing was possible; he had never seen a signpost or a speedometer marked in x's, nor yet a clock with y's on its dial. He thought Mr Wilkins might be interested to know this, and told him so.

Other boys raised questions which the master considered equally fatuous, and he was out of patience with the whole form by the time he had finished his explanation.

"We'll see how much you've taken in," he said. "You can work out the next one for yourselves." And he wrote a similar problem on the blackboard and sat down at the master's desk.

The problem again concerned a journey from one milestone to the next, and once more the data consisted of x's, with a few y's thrown in for good measure.

"Do we have to work it out in our books, sir?" inquired Martin-Jones.

"Of course. You don't imagine I want it embroidered on the lampshade, do you!" came the curt reply.

Temple put up his hand. "Please, sir, that sum's impossible to answer, sir. You haven't told us how far it is from one milestone to the next. We can't work it out until we know that, can we, sir?"

Mr Wilkins took a deep breath to cool the impatience rising inside him. "There would be little point, Temple, in having milestones that were not exactly one mile apart," he said, and left his desk to see how the back row were progressing. "Well, Bromwich, have you worked out how long it would take?"

"Yes, sir: three days, sir."

"Three days to go a mile! Don't be ridiculous, you silly little boy. Why, a snail could do it in that time!"

"I was pretending it *was* a snail, sir. The sum didn't say it had got to be a man, so I thought, now supposing this snail…"

"I… I… *Corwumph!*… Well, Darbishire! I suppose *you're* going to tell me you've worked it out in earwigs!"

"No, I used a proper man, sir, and it makes the sum come out much faster. According to my figures he must have finished the journey shortly after half-past z, sir."

Mr Wilkins drew in his breath like a vacuum-cleaner coping with an obstinate fluff-ball. Then he clasped his hand over his eyes and tottered blindly back to the master's desk. He stopped abruptly when he bumped into it, but the exercise must have made him feel better, for his tone was back to normal when next he spoke.

"Hands up all boys who have put down 'twenty minutes' for the answer."

No hands went up and Mr Wilkins began to simmer again. "This form needs waking up! Not one right answer to a perfectly straightforward sum. Very well. I'll have the whole lot of you in here at quarter-past four on Saturday and we'll go through the examples again."

Form Three received the news without enthusiasm. The 1st XI would be playing a "home" match on Saturday, which everybody would be required to watch; but when the game ended at half-past three, village leave would be granted. Mr Wilkins had purposely chosen an awkward hour for his detention class, for the journey to the village took ten minutes each way, and with so little time to spend when they got there, it would not be worth their while to go at all.

Jennings was not worried about missing village leave, for he had no money to spend, and anyway, he had planned to devote the time to finishing his life-stories for the magazine. Publication date had now been fixed for the following Tuesday and there was much work to be done.

The algebra lesson ended when the bell rang for break, and Mr Wilkins went along to the staff room for a well-earned cup of coffee.

"I've just about had enough of that Form Three," he confided to Mr Carter. "I gave them a simple problem this morning and the whole lot behaved like half-wits – if that! Still, they're not going to get away with it. I shall make them sit up on Saturday afternoon, believe me!"

The second post had just arrived, and on the mantelpiece was a letter addressed to L P Wilkins, Esq., in his sister's writing. Most unexpected, he thought, as he tore open the envelope: for his younger sister, Margaret, was usually too busy nursing at a London hospital to spare much time for correspondence with her brother. He was very fond of his sister, which was not surprising, for she was a very likeable person. He unfolded the sheet of notepaper and read:

Dear Lance,

I shall be spending next weekend with some friends near Brighton, so I thought it would be a good opportunity to break my journey and look in to see you for an hour or so about tea-time on Saturday. I gather I can catch a bus from Dunhambury to Linbury, but don't bother to meet me; I expect I shall be able to find my own way.

Love,

Margaret.

He folded the letter and put it back in the envelope as one of the other masters drew near. It would never do for his colleagues to find out that his first name was Lancelot. Naturally the Headmaster knew, and so did Mr Carter, for few facts escaped *his* attention: but so far as the school in general was concerned, L P Wilkins preferred to be known by his initials.

Not that there was anything *wrong* with Lancelot: it was a splendid name for the right sort of person, but somehow Mr Wilkins felt that the right person was not him. Had his name been Bill or Jack or Tom, he would have made no secret of it. But Lancelot...oh, no!

On the staff room noticeboard was a list of the masters' duties, from which he learned that Mr Carter would be in charge of the school on Saturday afternoon and evening. That fitted in excellently: the detention class would be over by quarter-past five and he would then be free to entertain his sister and show her round the building.

Most of the masters drifted out of the staff room when they had drunk their coffee, and only Mr Wilkins and Mr Carter were left, when a knock sounded on the door a few minutes before the end of break.

The visitor was Jennings – feeling a little uncertain of the reception that awaited him.

"It's about our magazine, sir," he explained. "I'm writing the lives of famous characters like Oliver Cromwell and people, sir, but we thought chaps might get a bit bored reading them, so we're going to put in a few *in*-famous characters as well – like you and Mr Wilkins, sir. Or rather," he amended hastily as a loud "Corwumph!" came from the direction of the mantelpiece, "I should say, characters who are not quite so famous as Oliver Cromwell, but are more interesting to read about."

"Go on," said Mr Carter in the resigned voice of one who sees difficulties ahead.

"Well, sir, masters never tell people what *they* were like when they were at school, or whether they had any exciting adventures before they grew old; and those are just the sort of things that'd go down ever so well in a wall-newspaper, sir."

Mr Wilkins grunted his disapproval. "I'm not having anecdotes of my nursery days stuck up all over the common room, thanks very much."

"I see, sir." Jennings braced himself and took a deep breath because he knew that his next question might not be well received. "Well, sir, perhaps we could manage to write a chatty paragraph if we just knew what your initials stood for, sir."

A deeper shade of pink suffused Mr Wilkins' cheek. "My name, little boy, is L P Wilkins. And what LP stands for is not your business."

Jennings shuffled uncomfortably at the rebuke. "No, sir, of course not. Sorry, sir."

He had not meant the question to sound impudent, but it seemed that he was skating on thin ice so far as Mr Wilkins was concerned. Perhaps Mr Carter would be more helpful: there was no secret about *his* name because he signed himself Michael Carter quite openly in autograph books. His age, of course, was another matter and it would be futile, as well as bad manners, to ask what it was, considering that grown-ups always gave some impossible answer such as a hundred and six last birthday. On the other hand, some vague clue would be useful to a biographer and, with some diffidence, Jennings suggested this.

"What sort of a clue?" asked Mr Carter, puzzled.

"Well, like, say, for instance, sir, whether you can remember the first motor-car, or if you were alive before they invented television."

Unlike his colleague, Mr Carter was more amused than annoyed. He thought for a few moments and said: "Well, Jennings, Mr Wilkins has been telling me that Form Three maths needs more practice, so try working this out. Five years ago, I was twice as old as you will be in four years' time, and in ten years' time I shall be five times older than you were two years ago."

He said it so rapidly that Jennings blinked and said: "Oh, golly, sir. I'll have an awful job scrubbing round that one. It's worse than the sums about the chap charging along at x miles an hour, sir."

Another grunt of disapproval came from the region of the mantelpiece. "I suggest, Jennings, that you stop being inquisitive. If you've nothing better to do than waste our time asking a lot of silly questions, you'd better run along."

ANTHONY BUCKERIDGE

As Jennings left the room he couldn't help thinking that the campaign to make Mr Wilkins happier was not making much progress. Why, the man was growing even more surly if that were possible!

The bell for the next lesson sounded and he hurried back to his classroom to find Darbishire impatiently awaiting the result of the interview.

"Did you get anything out of them, Jen?"

"Not a thing! Tight as limpets, both of them. I'll just have to put something like *Mr Michael Carter is a gentleman of riper years whose age is a problem for mathematicians*."

"And what about Old Wilkie?"

"He's worse. His past is obscure and he doesn't want it talked about."

They sat down at their desks and opened their books for the Headmaster's Latin lesson. While they were waiting, Jennings scanned his list of the famous and not so famous. It bore the names:

J Caesar.

Sir F Drake.

Mr M Carter.

Messrs O Cromwell and L P Wilkins, Esq.

The late Dr A Grimshaw (deceased?).

Presently he said: "I wish I knew what LP stood for."

"Lowest prices – loose pages – long playing – lost property," hazarded Darbishire, looking up from his reading of the late doctor's *Latin Grammar*.

"Oh, don't talk such antiseptic eyewash, Darbi! How could he have a name like Lost Property?"

"Who?"

"Mr Wilkins, of course."

"Oh, sorry, I didn't know you meant him. You just asked what it stood for."

But there seemed no way of finding out, and by tea time Jennings had almost decided to scrap his life-stories of the less famous and stick to people like O Cromwell, Esq.

At least, he knew what the O stood for!

14

Venables Stands Treat

It was just after lunch on Friday that Venables sprang his pleasant surprise. The idea came to him quite suddenly as he was on his way up to the common room. He was pretending to be an articulated lorry at the time, and the first sign that Jennings and Darbishire had of his approach was the roar of internal combustion rattling through his vocal cords as he manoeuvred the imaginary vehicle through the narrow doorway and parked it in a one-way street behind the ping-pong table.

"You're just the characters I'm looking for," he began, as soon as he had switched off his engine with a nerve-shattering clearance of his throat. "I've decided to do you a supersonic favour because you've been pretty decent to me lately."

The pretty decent ones exchanged surprised glances. "Have we?" asked Jennings.

"Oh, yes! I haven't forgotten how you presented me with my Latin book the other week, and on top of that, Darbi let me scrape out his empty jam pot at tea, last Tuesday."

"Oh, forget it," replied Darbishire generously. "Any time I've got a pot going begging with nothing in it, you're quite welcome to the scrapings."

It was then that Venables outlined his plans for the big treat. By the morning's post he had received fifty pence from his

154

uncle, with instructions to spend it sensibly and not squander it on selfish pleasure. And what, Venables had asked himself, could be more sensible than investing part of it in a few well-chosen doughnuts? Surely, no one could accuse him of indulging in selfish pleasure if he invited two friends, renowned for their decency, to join him!

"So I thought, how would it be if we all three beetled down to old Mrs Lumley's home-made cake and bicycle shop during village leave tomorrow afternoon," he went on. "She's got fizzy drinks in all colours and her supersonic home-made doughnuts are quite famous in cake-eating circles."

"Coo, thanks very much, Venables – that'd be smashing!"

The guests shook their host's hand like a pump-handle and thumped him on the back as though spring-cleaning a carpet. And Jennings added: "I've always liked you, Venables. Haven't I always said so, Darbi? Haven't you often heard me say that old Venables is a…"

Suddenly he stopped and the carpet cleaning ceased in mid-beat. "Wait a sec. though; we're all being kept in for old Wilkie at quarter-past four tomorrow."

The announcement came as a jet of water on the leaping flames of their joy. "Oh, fish-hooks, I'd forgotten about that! We'll have to call the whole thing off, then," said the host gloomily.

"Oh, no! Don't be such a mouldy cad, Venables," cried Darbishire in dismay. "Couldn't we go next week instead?"

Venables was willing to postpone the feast, but Jennings vetoed the suggestion with some vigour. It occurred to him that if their host's enthusiasm was given a breathing-space, the invitation might not be repeated. A week was a long time: long enough for warm feelings of generosity to congeal into a jelly of indifference; long enough for the money to be spent on

ANTHONY BUCKERIDGE

other things. Why, there was no knowing *what* might happen if the treat was postponed for a week.

"I vote we go tomorrow," he said firmly. "We'll have masses of time if we beetle off as soon as the match is over. Old Wilkie ought to be pleased, really, because we'll have more strength to cope with all that *x* and *y* caper if we've just done a spot of refuelling on ginger-pop and stuff."

They went into the matter in some detail. Allowing ten minutes each way for travelling, they would still have a clear twenty for the feast. That, surely, would be ample time!

"All right, then; we'll do that," Venables agreed. "But we mustn't hang about and waste time. We'll have to keep up a steady *x* plus *y* miles an hour all the way down to the village."

On Saturday morning the weather was cold and damp, but it cleared slightly by lunch time and the 1st XI match was played with a pale sun shining overhead.

Jennings, Darbishire and Venables stood on the touchline with sixty-five of their colleagues and cheered the remaining eleven on to victory. The game ended on the stroke of half-past three, and ten minutes later Venables was leading his panting guests along the village street to where a notice in a cottage window said: *Chas. Lumley – Home-made Cakes and Bicycles Repaired.*

"Here we are," said Venables, pushing open the garden gate. "Of course, it's only a little place. If it was a smart restaurant they wouldn't bother about repairing home-made cakes."

The Lumley catering and engineering organisation was conducted on a modest scale, and the firm's chief business consisted of old Mrs Lumley serving cakes and minerals in the front parlour, while Chas. repaired punctures in the garden shed.

There was not much room in the parlour and on the rare occasions when customers called for refreshment, they would sit round the little table in the window, after carefully shooing a cat from each chair and removing Mr Lumley's spare waistcoats from the chair-backs.

The three boys hurried into the cottage and threaded their way to the table through the gaps in the furniture.

"Make yourselves comfortable," Venables invited generously as he sat down. "It's my fifty pence and you've got my permish to go ahead and order anything you like – except a home-made bicycle."

"Coo, thanks," beamed Darbishire, edging his way onto a chair which was already occupied by a large black cat. "Good puss, good puss!" he said: which was not strictly true, for the cat stuck out its claws and hissed at him. As it was unwilling to move, he had to balance himself on the rim of the chair and remember not to lean back.

Mrs Lumley plodded heavily out of the kitchen to welcome her first customers of the day.

"Yerse?" she inquired.

"A plate of home-made cakes and doughnuts and three bottles of fizzy ginger-pop, please," Venables ordered importantly after conferring with his guests.

Darbishire followed Mrs Lumley's slow plod back to the kitchen with anxious eyes. "I hope she steps on it," he observed.

"There won't be much left of the doughnuts if she does. She's got shoes like violin cases," Jennings pointed out.

"No, I mean I hope she steps on the gas and gets a move on; it's about a quarter to four already."

Mrs Lumley had not hurried for forty years and had no intention of doing so now. She pottered slowly around the kitchen gathering up doughnuts, washing out glasses and breaking off from time to time to see if the cats' supper was simmering nicely on the kitchen range. At last she returned to the front room and set plates and bottles on the table with an appetising clatter.

"Thanks awfully,' said the customers, and wasted no time in setting about their meal. The doughnuts were delicious, for there was no doubt that Mrs Lumley was a good cook.

"It doesn't come to more than fifty pence, does it?" asked Darbishire, with his mouth full of doughnut and his mind full of earnest resolutions not to put his host to too much expense.

"Oh, no! Twenty pence, that'll be," said Mrs Lumley. "But you needn't pay now, ducks. You get on and enjoy it. I'll be through in the kitchen if you want any more."

For three minutes the champing of jaws was the only sound in the room. Then Jennings said: "Aren't these cakes supersonic! I haven't tasted anything like them since I was young – well, younger than I am now, anyway."

"Yes, and it's smashing pop, too. It's jolly generous of you to treat us like this, Venables. My father says that a generous impulse is…"

Darbishire's voice trailed away and he stared at his host in alarm. "I say, Ven, what's the matter? Are you feeling all right?"

"Mm? What's that? Oh, yes, I'm all right, thanks," came from Venables in a faint, far-away sort of voice.

Jennings looked up from his plate and he, too, frowned in puzzled wonder. For their host's doughnut lay untasted on his plate and the pop level had not ebbed from the rim of his glass.

"What's up, Venables? Indigestion or something?"

"No, I'm all right, thanks. I just had a sudden thought – that's all."

"You needn't worry about the detention, if that's what's biting you. If we start back in about five minutes we shall have bags of time."

"It's not the detention," replied Venables. "It was when you asked the old girl how much the bill came to. I suddenly thought to myself: 'Gosh!' I thought."

He broke off, overcome by some emotion, and stared with unseeing eyes at a china dog on the mantelpiece.

"Well, go on," Jennings prompted. "What happened after you thought 'Gosh'?"

With an effort Venables pulled himself together. "Well, after I'd thought 'Gosh,' I thought a bit more and then I thought 'Golly!' I thought – I changed my jacket after lunch because Matron wanted to sew a button on."

"What about it?"

"Well, don't get in a flap; everything will come out all right in the end – I hope, but…"

Venables ran his tongue over his dry lips. It was clear that he was approaching the climax of his story. It came with a rush: "…you see it was then I remembered I'd left my fifty pence piece in my other jacket that Matron's got."

"What!"

"Super sorrow and all that. It was just an accidental bish."

"Oh, fish-hooks, this is frightful!" wailed Darbishire. "We're half-way through these cakes and drinks now. Why do these hoo-hahs always have to pick on us to happen to? I'm not old enough to cope with these catastroscopes."

For some seconds they sat and stared at one another while their minds grappled with the problem. Four doughnuts and two bottles of pop had already been consumed and they hadn't a penny between the three of them to pay the bill. What was to be done? Explain their plight to Mrs Lumley and ask to pay at a later date? Impossible! She looked the sort of woman who wouldn't have trusted her own grandmother, let alone strangers with hearty appetites and empty pockets.

"There's only one thing to be done," Jennings decided, and turned to his host. "You'll have to hoof back to school at something a jolly sight faster than x miles an hour, Ven, and get that fifty p piece from your other jacket; Darbi and I will sit here and go on eating as though nothing has happened until you get back. Whatever we do, we mustn't let Mrs Lumley smell a rat."

Then came the second difficulty. Venables' double journey and the final return of all three to school would normally take thirty minutes of brisk travelling. Darbishire looked at his watch: it was one minute to four.

"Sixteen minutes to zero hour, We'll never do it in the time!"

"Yes, we will if Ven runs like blinko. Fifteen minutes all told for hoofing and one minute to pay the bill. Go on, Venables, get weaving, for Pete's sake; we've already wasted nearly half our spare minute in talking about it."

The host zigzagged his way out past the clutter of furniture, and a moment later they saw him sprinting down the village street in his race against the clock. He ran with a long, loping stride which put new heart into the watchers at the window. Why, if he could keep up that pace for a mile, he would be there and back almost before they had finished their sixth doughnut... *If* he could keep it up!

Darbishire turned away from the window. "Eat up, Jennings; we mustn't let the old girl suspect anything. If she knew we were calmly putting ourselves outside all these doughnuts without a penny to pay for them, she'd go off pop."

Jennings nodded absently. He was wondering whether Venables would be able to get back with the money before they had finished the cakes on the plate. If not, they would have to order more – or be faced with the bill!

"We've got to keep up appearances, that's what we've got to do," Darbishire prattled on nervously. "My father says that appearances are deceptive, but..." He stopped as the kitchen door opened and Mrs Lumley appeared.

"Thought as how I heard the front door slam," she said.

"Yes, it was our friend. He's just gone outside for a little while to – er, to take some exercise. He'll be back soon," Jennings explained.

Mrs Lumley's eye fell upon the now empty cake plate. "Made short work of me doughnuts and no mistake. Are you going to settle up now, ducks, or do you want some more?"

Faced with an embarrassing alternative, Jennings made the only choice he could. "Well, yes, I suppose we'd better have a few more, I'm afraid – I mean, we'd like some very much."

"Right you are, ducks!" Mrs Lumley returned to the kitchen, and Darbishire turned to his friend with alarm in his eyes.

"You ancient historic monument, Jennings; what did you want to order more for?"

"I had to! You heard her ask if we were ready to pay. If we don't go on eating and drinking and pretending everything's all right, she'll smell a rat as sure as eggs."

"Yes, I know, but all the same…"

It was a rash move, and the thought of the risks involved destroyed the last traces of Darbishire's hearty appetite. "I shan't be able to enjoy the next lot at all. I shall be wondering about Venables all the time. Supposing he sprains his ankle?… Supposing something goes wrong?… Oh, golly, what a gum-tree we shouldn't half be up!"

"Don't be such a gloomy specimen, Darbi! He'll be back with the money in less than ten minutes, so nothing *can* go wrong. You see if I'm not right!"

While Venables was pounding along Linbury Lane, Mr Wilkins was rounding up Form Three for the detention class, for he was anxious to make a prompt start or, better still, to begin a few minutes early.

His sister's letter had not said what time she was coming, but he was assuming that she would arrive at about five o'clock. In that case he would have to dismiss his class before the full hour was up, so it was most important that no time should be wasted in getting down to work.

Form Three were more than willing to fall in with Mr Wilkins' wishes. They took the view that the sooner they started, the sooner the miserable business would be over and done with.

They sat down at their desks, and Mr Wilkins called the roll. It gave him no pleasure to find that there were three absentees.

"Tut-tut-tut! Why on earth can't everybody be ready, when I'm in a hurry," he complained.

"They've gone to the village, sir," Temple informed him. "But they said they would be back by quarter-past."

"Well, I'm not waiting all afternoon for them. If they're not here in a couple of minutes, I'll – I'll – well, they'd better look out!"

"Wouldn't it be better if *we* all looked out, sir?" Atkinson suggested. "Then we might be able to see them coming."

"No, it would not. Open your text-books at page fourteen and read through the example it gives." And Mr Wilkins strode from the room and made for the landing window to see if the missing boys were even now panting up the drive, eager to get to grips with algebraical problems.

They were not; but Mr Carter was coming up the stairs and had to stop and listen to an account of his colleague's difficulties.

"You see, the point is, Carter, that my sister's coming this afternoon, and I want to get this class off my hands before she arrives. If she turns up before I'm free, would you mind seeing that someone takes her up to my room? She's not been here before and she doesn't know her way about."

"Certainly," Mr Carter replied. "Would you like me to look after your class for you, in case she arrives early?"

162

"No, no. I shall have finished with them by five o'clock, if only I can get started. Trouble is, I'm three boys short, but as soon as…"

He broke off and listened, as a curious noise was wafted up the stairs from the hall below. It was a sound that might have been made by a lorry chugging up a steep gradient, a pressure cooker announcing that lunch was ready, or even a two-handled saw churning its way through a tree trunk.

In point of fact, it was none of these things. It was Venables gasping for breath, as he started on the last lap of his marathon run to Matron's room to retrieve his fifty pence.

"Ah, here's one of them coming now. Lucky for him! He's just in time." And Mr Wilkins called loudly: "Come along, Venables! Hurry up, boy, I've been waiting five minutes for you already."

The runner wheezed up the stairs and sagged exhausted against the banisters. His face was a brilliant scarlet; his hair and forehead were bathed in perspiration; his collar clung damply to his neck and his socks lay in folds about his ankles. His shoulders heaved: he could not speak.

"Glad to see you've been hurrying," said Mr Wilkins briskly. "Run along to the classroom and get your books out. I'm starting right away."

By this time his heart had stopped pounding and his breathing was again under control, Venables found himself sitting at his desk, while Mr Wilkins paced the classroom explaining the importance of x and the advantages of y. He was not pleased when a hand rose, and Venables said: "Please, sir, I can't come in to class just yet, sir."

"What do you mean – you *can't* come in? You *have* come in. And only just in time, too."

"I've got to go down to the village again, sir. It's urgent!"

"You'll do nothing of the sort."

163

"But, sir, I *must*. I've left Jennings and Darbishire down there."

Mr Wilkins bristled. *He'd* have something to say to those two gentlemen when they condescended to turn up!

"Can't I go and fetch them sir? They'll never get back without me."

"I… I… *Corwumph!* Are you trying to be funny, boy? They know their way back; they're not half-wits – well, they are, *practically*, but that's neither here nor there."

"But, sir, you must listen, sir. You see what happened was…"

"Be quiet, Venables! I don't want to hear another word. We've wasted enough time as it is."

Mr Wilkins glared angrily and turned three shades pinker. He was standing no nonsense from Venables – or from Jennings and Darbishire, either! Obviously the three of them had put their heads together and hatched a plot; all this nonsense about one of them going to fetch the others was merely an excuse to waste time and miss half the detention class. When the conspirators realised that their scheme had misfired, they'd come back, quickly enough! Mr Wilkins smiled grimly. *He* was not the sort of man to be taken in by childish pranks!

"But, sir, it's urgent, sir! You don't understand."

"Silence, boy!" roared Mr Wilkins in a voice of thunder. "Don't you dare argue with me. You'll do as you're told, or it'll be the worse for the three of you!"

Venables shrugged helplessly. He had done his best in the teeth of fierce opposition. He felt sorry for Jennings and Darbishire but, after all, what more could *he* do about it?

15

The Paying Guest

There are times when an unkind Fate will swoop down upon its prey like a goshawk; at others, it will play a cat-and-mouse game with its victims' dwindling hopes. Upon Jennings and Darbishire awaiting the hour of liberation in Mrs Lumley's cottage, Fate used its delayed action technique and withheld until too late the sad news that Venables was not coming back.

For the first ten minutes after his departure they kept their fingers crossed and went on eating doughnuts. For a further five, they tapped their feet and fidgeted – to the annoyance of the cat population who were trying to sleep.

By quarter-past four they knew that their host had failed them and that trouble lay ahead in the stern shape of Mr Wilkins. But it was not until twenty-eight minutes past the hour that they realised what deeper troubles were even now at their door in the portly shape of Mrs Lumley. For stacked upon the table were the plates and bottles which they had felt obliged to order in their attempt to keep up appearances and stave off the evil moment when the bill would have to be paid.

"Why doesn't Venables *come!*" moaned Darbishire for the fifth time in three minutes.

"If you ask me, he's a treacherous traitor," Jennings retorted angrily. "Wait till I see him again! I'll make him live to regret it!"

"When *I* get hold of him, he'll regret it, but he may not live – not more than long enough to regret it, anyway."

It was not often that Darbishire bore ill-will towards his fellow-creatures, but now he was shocked beyond measure by what he imagined to be Venables' heartless conduct. A nice sort of treat this was turning out to be! He looked at the table with a jaundiced eye.

"Have another doughnut, Jen? There's just one left."

"Golly, no, I couldn't. I should burst. I've had about seven already and four bottles of ginger-pop."

"It's time we got cracking and asked for some more, all the same. We haven't had a fresh lot for ages and ages and she's beginning to give us those funny looks again. If she smells a rat, we're sunk, don't forget!"

Jennings groaned quietly. "I know, I know! But it's got past smelling a rat by this time. She'll be sending for the Pied Piper of Hamelin or the corporation rodent inspector if we don't do something about it soon."

There was no denying that Mrs Lumley had been looking at them curiously for some little time, but this was due to sheer surprise. Never had she seen so few boys eat so many doughnuts; and little did she know that each mouthful nearly choked them!

"Oh fish-hooks! She's coming back again. Try and look hungry, Darbi!" Jennings whispered, as the kitchen door opened with a squeak.

"You can't look hungry when you've just had to loosen your belt," Darbishire complained. He shook his head sadly, for he was very fond of home-made cakes and would often lie awake at night wondering what it must be like to eat so many that he just couldn't eat any more. Now, he knew!

"Tut-tut! Well, I never!" exclaimed Mrs Lumley, eyeing the cluttered table. "You lads have got an appetite, that I *will* say. I don't think you'd better 'ave no more, or you'll be queer. Let's see now, that's fourteen cakes and doughnuts you've had altogether, and seven bottles of fizz – er, that'll be, er – forty-seven *p*."

Jennings shifted uncomfortably in his chair. The time had come to explain and it was not going to be easy.

"I'm afraid there's been a bit of a bish," he began.

"There's been a *what*, ducks?"

"There's been a sort of accidental mistake – quite by accident, of course. You see…"

Mrs Lumley checked the bill. "No, ducks; there's no mistake. Forty-seven *p* it'll cost you, though where you've found room to put it all is more than…"

Darbishire had been staring out of the window with glassy eyes. Suddenly he gave a convulsive start and crowed, "Wacko!" For he had heard the click of the garden gate and had caught a glimpse of a human shape behind the holly bush.

His heart leapt with joy. Venables was coming back! Good old Venables! He had not failed them after all! Mindless of Mrs Lumley's bewildered expression, he leaned across the table and whispered the glad tidings in Jennings' ear.

"Oh, goodo!" cried Jennings. "We're saved, then! And we're still three *p* inside the limit."

Good old Venables! The chap must be hungry after his long journey: it was only fair that he should be allowed to enjoy the last three pence worth of his uncle's present. Jennings turned to Mrs Lumley.

"If you don't mind, we'll just have a last plate of doughnuts for our friend, please."

167

"But I thought as how he'd gone."

"Yes, but he's come back. Just a last three *p* worth for the road, and then we'll be off."

As Mrs Lumley returned to the kitchen, the front door opened and the two boys leapt to their feet to greet their long-lost host.

"I say, Venables, you have been a…"

Jennings' voice clicked off suddenly like an unpopular radio programme. For the door had opened to admit a complete stranger.

The newcomer was an attractive young lady in her early twenties. She was slim and fair, with a gay sparkle in her eyes and a friendly smile about her lips. She was smiling now as she set down her suitcase and said: "Do you mind if I join you at your table? There doesn't seem to be anywhere else to sit."

"Um? Oh, yes, please do; that'll be all right; delighted," mumbled Jennings in a daze; and he made a movement to clear the crockery from the place where Venables had sat.

Darbishire, too, had risen to greet his host and now leaned weakly against the mantelpiece muttering to himself: "*Not* Venables! Oh, my goodness, it isn't Venables! All that hoping we were saved and now it isn't Venables after all!"

"Be quiet, and pull yourself together, you coot! You're chuntering like a village idiot," Jennings told him in a warning whisper. "You needn't go on and *on* saying who it isn't. We know by now, and anyway, it's not polite."

He turned back to the young lady and gallantly removed a struggling ginger cat from her chair.

All the same, he could sympathise with his friend's shocked reaction, for this new development was enough to numb the nerves of the strongest. And to make matters worse, they had just ordered a further supply of doughnuts in celebration!

"You seem to have been doing yourselves well," said the young lady, waving a hand towards the empty plates and bottles.

Jennings nodded. "We – well, we sort of had no choice, if you see what I mean."

The newcomer looked at the boys with interest. She had often heard her brother speak of the amount of food which schoolboys were reputed to eat, but she had never really believed him.

The boys, for their part, looked at the newcomer with no interest at all; she seemed a poor substitute for Venables and his fifty pence. They noticed, of course, that she was young and attractive. They even noticed the initials *MW* on her suitcase, but this rang no bell in their minds; and, indeed, there was no reason why it should have done, because there was little family resemblance between Margaret Wilkins and her elder brother, Lancelot.

She was slim and he was burly; she was soft of speech and light on her feet, whereas her brother had a voice like a loud-hailer and footsteps which echoed like a deep-sea diver marking time with his boots on. In character, the two differed just as widely, and Margaret regarded her brother's turbulent manner with quiet amusement. In spite of this, however, they managed to remain on the friendliest of terms.

Although Jennings and Darbishire noticed nothing unusual about Miss Wilkins, she could see at a glance that something was very much the matter with *them*; and when the new consignment of cakes had arrived and she had ordered a cup of tea for herself, she said: "You don't look very cheerful. Aren't you going to eat these cakes she's just brought?"

"No thanks," Jennings answered weakly. "If I looked another doughnut in the face, I should explode."

"Something's gone wrong, hasn't it?" she asked.

169

ANTHONY BUCKERIDGE

They nodded miserably.

"Won't you tell me what the matter is? I might be able to help."

Jennings shook his head. "It's very decent of you, but I don't think you could. There's only one person who could help us, and he's not here. He invited us out to a special feast, and just as we were halfway through the first plateful he had to go and think 'Gosh!'"

Miss Wilkins looked puzzled. "He had to go and do *what*?"

"Oh, he didn't really have to go anywhere to think it. He just sat there where you're sitting now and thought it. And after he'd thought 'Gosh!' once or twice, he calmly turned round and told us he'd left his rhino behind."

"His rhino? Does he work in a zoo?"

"Oh, no: Jennings means his money," Darbishire explained. "And he didn't actually turn *round* and tell us, because he was facing us all the time."

"Well, you know what I mean," said Jennings.

"Oh, yes, *I* do, but perhaps this lady doesn't. She might think he hadn't got the face to tell us so he swooshed round and looked out of the window."

"I think I understand – so far," said Margaret. "Won't you go on?"

And by degrees she coaxed more of the story from them and learned who they were and which school they came from.

"...and of course, it may not really be all Venables' fault." Jennings finished up. "Because there's a mouldy detention class we're supposed to have gone to, and if he's been nabbed for that we shall have to go on eating for simply hours and hours yet – perhaps all night even!"

Miss Wilkins sympathised. The prospect of continual doughnut-eating to allay Mrs Lumley's suspicions was too

170

horrible to think about. She suggested a remedy: "If you can't leave till the bill's paid, perhaps you'll let me pay it for you."

"Good gracious, no; we couldn't possibly!" Jennings protested. "We wouldn't dream of taking money from you. After all, you're practically our guest; we invited you to sit at our table."

Margaret changed her line of approach. "We could call it a loan. Then you'll be able to go back to school and repay me when you've found your friend."

A loan from a guest! Jennings didn't like the idea at first, but there seemed no other solution.

"Well, all right, then; thank you very much," he said. "You could be a sort of *paying* guest, couldn't you? And we'll let you have it back the minute we've seen Venables – if he's still alive after Old Wilkie's finished with him."

"Who?" she inquired.

"Old Wilkie – Mr Wilkins by rights; he's one of our masters and he goes berserk and charges about like a fire-breathing dragon when he's in a bate."

"Really!" Margaret raised an interested eyebrow. It was obvious from the way he spoke that the boy had no idea he was addressing the fire-breathing dragon's sister. She was about to enlighten him when he hurried on: "Yes, honestly! You'd never believe the chronic hoo-hahs Old Wilkie kicks up unless you'd sat through one of his mouldy algebra lessons. And it's no good trying to be decent to him – he just goes into the attack like an armoured column and won't listen. I've met some frantic types in my time, but Old Wilkie – phew!"

It was not, Miss Wilkins decided, a good moment to claim kinship to an armoured column. After all, a guest – even though only a paying one – should not embarrass her hosts when they had troubles enough already. All the same, she could not help feeling rather surprised at Jennings' description. She knew her brother was inclined to be explosive when things went wrong at home, but she had never given much thought to the way in which he dealt with his boys at school.

So, wisely, she changed the subject, and as the boys seemed in some hurry to be gone, she drank up her tea and asked whether she might walk back to school with them.

"Righto! Then we can give you the money," said Darbishire. "Of course, it's probably taking you out of your way. I hope you won't mind."

"Oh, no, I'm going to Linbury Court in any case. I'm calling to see someone. In fact, I should have been there by now, but I wasn't sure of the way and I got off the bus in the village, by mistake."

Darbishire looked at her in some surprise. Was she a parent?

"If you don't mind my saying so, you look a bit young to be some chap's mother," he said politely.

"No, I'm not that. I'm – er, I'm some chap's sister."

She called to Mrs Lumley for the bill and suggested that they should take the remaining doughnuts back to school for Venables. They agreed with some reluctance, for Venables was not a very popular character with either of them just then.

"Fifty-three pence, all told, ducks," said Mrs Lumley. "Three for the tea and fifty for the rest. And if these here lads gets the colly-wobbles after all that lot, don't say as I never warned you."

They set off along the village street, Jennings carrying Margaret's suitcase and Darbishire carrying the spare doughnuts in a paper bag. They were deeply grateful to their paying guest and thanked her a dozen times for coming to their rescue. But behind their gratitude lurked the thought of what was going to happen when they got back to school.

It was nearly five o'clock by now and they would have missed most of the detention class – perhaps all of it! What on earth would Mr Wilkins say!

Margaret sensed their worry and asked them questions about the more pleasant side of school life to keep their minds off their immediate future. They told her about the *Form Three Times* and the trouble they were having with the forthcoming number: which brought the conversation back to the delicate topic of Mr Wilkins.

"I'm sure he's not really such a monster as you make out," said Margaret, after listening to a catalogue of her brother's shortcomings.

"Oh, but he is – he's worse!" Darbishire confirmed. "He's not like the other masters at all. Now Mr Carter's jolly decent; so's Mr Hind and even the Archbeako – he's the Head you know – even *he's* more or less human when he's in the mood. But Old Wilkie – well, I ask you!"

Margaret felt that the discussion had gone so far that it might as well be thrashed out properly. Perhaps, from her deeper knowledge of Mr Wilkins, she might be able to put matters right.

"But what exactly is it that you don't like about him?" she asked.

"Well, we don't mind him barking at us when we've done something wrong – we do, sometimes," Darbishire admitted. "But it's just the same when we're trying to be decent. Take the other day, for instance: Jennings wanted to have a bash at writing the life-stories of famous and unfamous characters, like, say, Mr Carter and Mr Wilkins for this magazine we told you about. You know – what they were like when they were young, and what their full names were."

"We know Mr Wilkins' initials are LP, but what *that* stands for is a mystery," Jennings added. "I doubt if anyone knows really."

Margaret smiled. So Lancelot was secretive about his romantic Christian name! That was another thing she hadn't known before.

"Of course, we didn't dare ask him how old he was," Jennings went on. "He's not the sort of chap you can ask questions like that."

"And did Mr Carter tell you his age?"

"Well, no, actually, he didn't, but we could find out if we wanted to, because he's got to the sort of age you can only work out by algebra," Jennings explained.

"Good gracious! That sounds terribly ancient."

"Well, you know, you need x's and y's like the old geologist geezers use for finding out how old fossils and things are. Mind you, I don't mean Mr Carter's as old as all that, but I bet he's at least thirty."

He prattled on about the responsibilities of editing a high-class magazine and touched lightly upon the trials of press photography and the imperfections of the *Ideal Junior Printing Outfit.*

"Your magazine sounds splendid to me," said Miss Wilkins. "We must have a chat about it before I go. Perhaps I could help you with a few ideas."

The boys thought the suggestion extremely unlikely – coming as it did from one who was merely "some chap's sister" – but they were too polite to say so.

They had reached the school gates by this time and their uneasiness increased as they went up the drive.

"We'd better say goodbye now," said Jennings. "I'll get Venables to bring that money to you, because I don't suppose we'll see you again before you go."

Margaret was sorry to hear it. "But aren't we going to have a chat about your magazine?" she asked.

Jennings shook his head. "I don't see how we can. You see, being stranded in the village means we've missed the detention class."

"Is that serious?"

"*Is* that serious! Is *that* serious! Old Wilkie will be in such a bate he'll – well, if you hear a supersonic explosion in about five minutes' time, you'll know we've just reported to him."

"You ought to hear Jennings' famous imitation of Mr Wilkins' getting in a bate and going off pop," said Darbishire. "Do it, Jen! It's good enough for television, really it is!"

"I wouldn't say that," replied Jennings modestly. "It's just a little thing I worked out. It goes like this." He held his breath until he was red in the face and then, with arms flailing like a windmill, he burst out: "I... I... *Corwumph!* I've had enough of this trumpery moonshine, you uncouth youth, you...you *silly little boy!*"

"I should never have believed it," said Margaret solemnly.

"Oh yes you would, if you'd ever seen Mr Wilkins – it's just like him," Darbishire assured her. "It's taken ten months of practice to get it right." He smiled his congratulations to the impersonator and then turned again to the paying guest. "By the way, who is it you've come to see? We could round him up for you if you like."

"Don't bother, I'll find my way about."

"Well, don't go wandering into Mr Wilkins' room by mistake, if you want to get off the premises in one piece," Jennings advised. "He'll be hopping mad by this time and just ripe for the big explosion."

At that moment, Mr Carter came out of the front door and made his way down the steps and across the quad towards them.

175

"Good afternoon; my name's Carter," he said. "You must be Miss Wilkins, I imagine."

Margaret admitted her identity with a smile.

"I'm glad you found your way safely," said Mr Carter. "If you'll come along with me, I'll take you up to your brother's room. I promised to look out for you, because he's been busy with a detention class, but he'll be free in a moment."

From the corner of his eye Mr Carter noticed a strangeness in the manner of Jennings and Darbishire. They stood rigid as though in a trance, pink of face with open mouths and staring eyes. Jennings dropped the visitor's suitcase as though the handle was red-hot, while Darbishire's fingers made little twitching movements on the small paper bag he held in his palsied grasp.

Mr Carter turned hurriedly away from the unnerving sight. Why must boys always choose a moment when guests were present to look as though they were suffering from sunstroke and delayed concussion, he wondered? He picked up the suitcase and led the way up the steps.

"It must be some time since you've seen your brother," he said. "I expect you'll have plenty to talk about."

Her reply sounded clear and distinct in the ears of the spellbound audience at the foot of the steps.

"Yes, rather! There's quite a lot I'm just dying to tell him," she said.

16

Visitor for Mr Wilkins

Anyone who has stepped under an ice-cold shower-bath under the impression that it was a hot one, will know something of the shock that Jennings and Darbishire felt when they realised that their paying guest was a close relative of Mr Wilkins.

For a few seconds after Mr Carter had closed the front door, the two boys stood riveted to the ground with horrified surprise. Then, in a strained, unnatural voice, Darbishire said: "I just can't believe it! I simply *cannot* believe it! I feel faint; I should collapse if it wasn't for all these doughnuts inside me. Old Wilkie's sister, of all people! And we've gone and put both feet *slap-bang-plonk* into the stickiest bish in history."

It is doubtful whether Jennings heard him, for his mind was reeling at the thought of the terrible thing he had done: all those pointed remarks about fire-breathing dragons; and, worse still, the famous imitation of L P Wilkins, Esq., in a bate! What must she have thought!

"Why *ever* couldn't she have told us she was his sister in the first place!" he demanded. "It was a mouldy trick keeping quiet about it and letting us go on talking."

"M'yes, but I *do* see her point," Darbishire replied reasonably. "If Old Wilkie was my brother I shouldn't be so proud of it that I'd want to go round telling every stranger I

177

met. What worries me is how we're going to face him, now she's gone and told him everything."

Steeped in gloom they made their way indoors and hung their caps and coats in the changing-room. The detention class had just been dismissed and the corridors were alive with third-formers, their heads still swimming with algebraic problems

"You two are going to get your chips all right," Temple prophesied as he met them on the stairs. "Old Wilkie was as livid as mud when you didn't turn up. He nearly went off pop."

"Don't talk to me about going off pop – I've just had seven doughnuts." Darbishire thrust the paper bag into Temple's hands. "Here you are – eat these! We *were* going to give them to Venables, but I don't feel like being decent to him just at present."

It was growing dark now, but through the window, Jennings could just make out the form of their late host, hurrying over the quad towards the drive at the same record-breaking pace he had shown an hour earlier. He must be stopped at once, Jennings decided: and calling to Darbishire, he dashed out of the building in pursuit.

Venables had nearly reached the end of the drive when he heard the shouts behind him and came to a halt. He seemed surprised when he saw who his pursuers were.

"Oh, there you are! How did you get back? I was just hoofing down to Old Mother Lumley's to liberate you. I've got my fifty pence, now, look."

"You're a mouldy cad, Venables – leaving us stranded in the middle of all those doughnuts," Jennings cried as he bounded up to the would-be rescuer. "We had to eat the whole fifty *p*'s worth and you can jolly well fork out the cash."

Venables looked alarmed. "Oh heavens, no! I only meant to spend half that, even when I was with you. And now I haven't had any and you've got out anyway, it's not fair to expect me to fork out at all."

In vain they reasoned with him as they retraced their steps up the drive; but Venables was not interested in their private debts and maintained that they had had no right to spend on such a lavish scale.

"Well, you shouldn't have pushed off and left us," Jennings argued. "We've been exposed to the most frantic dangers, what with Old Wilkie gunning for us because we weren't there, and Old Mrs Lumley after us because we still *were*. And what's more we've got indigestion, and on top of that our paying guest's turned out to be a wolf in the grass."

"You mean a snake in the grass," corrected Darbishire, who liked to have things right, even at times of crisis. "My father says it's wolves who go about in sheep's clothing."

"What do they want to do that for?"

"Oh, they don't really!"

"You said they *did*."

"Ah, but that was just a saying. You don't actually find wolves wearing sheepskin waistcoats and things, any more than you really have snakes in the grass."

"But you *do* have snakes in the grass. Where else would you expect to find grass snakes?"

"Well, I wouldn't expect to find them in Mrs Lumley's tea shop pretending to be angels in disguise, and being Mr Wilkins' sister all the time."

The conversation seemed to be drifting away from the point, which was that their next move must be in the direction of Mr Wilkins' study. Their hearts quailed at the prospect – not because of the punishment which they might well expect for missing the detention class, but because *she* would be there.

She would have told him all by this time. Why, she might even make them repeat their rash words or… But, no… Never again, Jennings felt, could he bring himself to utter the words of his famous impersonation.

They left Venables in the hall and slowly, very slowly, mounted the stairs. At the top, they sat down on a laundry basket; they felt they needed a five-minute break to gather strength for the ordeal which lay before them.

"Bags you knock and go in first when we get there," Darbishire urged. "I shouldn't have the strength. My mind's wobbling too much at the thought of her actually sitting there, at this very moment, and telling Mr Wilkins everything we said about him."

The boys would have been surprised if they could have seen Miss Margaret Wilkins at that very moment. Admittedly, she was sitting in the armchair in her brother's study, but if she intended to pour forth outraged complaints she was taking a long time to set about it. Instead, she sipped a cup of tea and ate the crumpets which he had prepared specially in her honour.

"It's quite a change to see you in these surroundings," she said. "But you shouldn't have gone to all this trouble, Lancelot. I had a cup of tea before I arrived."

He looked up sharply at the mention of his Christian name.

"If you don't mind, Margaret, we'll leave the *Lancelot* out of it; I don't want it broadcast."

"But why not? You've always been Lancelot at home."

That, Mr Wilkins explained, was different. At home, his name sounded perfectly natural, but if it was to be bandied about the school he would never know a moment's peace.

"What shall I call you then – Old Wilkie?"

"I – er, well, it's better than Lancelot, anyway. It's what the boys call me, when I'm not supposed to be listening. You can leave out the 'Old' though; it's just a sort of courtesy title."

He jabbed the toasting fork into a crumpet and held it in front of the fire. Margaret watched him with interest. Was he really as heartless as the boys made out? She had always thought of him as a simple soul beneath his bluff exterior. A little forthright, perhaps, but…

"Have another cup of tea!" invited the simple soul.

"No, thanks, Lance – er, Wilkie. I had some in the village with two of your boys. Jennings and Darbishire they said their names were. I thought they were rather nice."

"What!"

The toasting fork quivered like a harp-string and the crumpet fell into the fire with a sizzle, as Mr Wilkins leapt to his feet and stared at his sister in surprise.

"You…you mean to tell me – well, dash it all, Margaret, this is a fine thing! They were supposed to be in my detention class – not guzzling food with my own sister. So that's where they were! They're going to find themselves in so much trouble they'll begin to wish…"

"But it wasn't their fault! They were frightfully upset about missing your class, but they were stranded without any money."

Mr Wilkins was not impressed. He stopped staring and turned to cope with the flaming crumpet which was filling the room with a pungent smell of roasted dough. He tried to spear it with the toasting fork, but only succeeded in knocking it farther into the fire; which did nothing to improve the state of his feelings. Curtly, he told his sister that in matters of school discipline he was not prepared to listen to excuses from an outsider. Jennings and Darbishire would be severely punished – and that was that!

He was rather surprised, therefore, when she asked whether she could see them again before she left. "What on earth do you want to do that for?" he demanded.

"I promised to give them some suggestions for their magazine," she explained. "I gather you weren't very helpful when they wanted to write your life-story."

"I should think not, indeed. My life-story! Never heard such trumpery moonshine. Anyway, they've had to think again because I didn't tell them anything."

"That's why I want to see them. I could tell them all sorts of interesting things."

There was a hint of mischief in Margaret's voice which made him look at her with sudden misgiving as she went on: "Do you remember that time when you were very small and you had six helpings of Christmas pudding? I remember father saying, 'Lancelot, my boy, let this be a lesson to you never to…"

"For heaven's sake!" Mr Wilkins' voice rose in wild alarm. "You'd never tell them a thing like that; don't be such a rotter, Margaret!"

She smiled and repeated his words: " 'Don't be such a rotter, Margaret!' I remember your saying that, years ago, when you fell out of the apple tree onto the compost heap and got your best suit dirty. Now I come to think of it, that wouldn't make a bad story, either."

"I… I…but dash it all, Margaret, you know perfectly well that wasn't my fault. The branch was rotten – it let me down."

"It wasn't the boys' fault that they didn't turn up for your class. Their friend let *them* down."

Mr Wilkins blinked in amazement. He had been looking forward to entertaining his sister to tea and crumpets, and chatting pleasantly of family matters. Well, they were chatting of family matters right enough, he told himself, but hardly in the way he had been expecting. Besides, it was sheer nonsensical tomfoolery to compare his unfortunate mishap in the apple tree all those years ago with Jennings and Darbishire missing his detention class. It wasn't the same thing at all, and the sooner Margaret realised it, the better.

But she *wouldn't* realise it! "It's exactly the same sort of thing," she argued. "They were both the silly kind of accident that boys are always getting involved in. And if you can't see it now, try reading about it in the life-story of Lancelot Phineas Wilkins, Esq., when it comes out in the next number of the *Form Three Times!*"

Mr Wilkins rocked top-heavily on his heels and clutched at the bookcase for support. "I... I... *Corwumph!* But Margaret, you couldn't... You *wouldn't*..."

She nodded. She could... She *would!*

The crumpet had burnt itself to a cinder and mechanically Mr Wilkins opened the window to let in a breath of fresh air. He felt he needed air; preferably a cool current playing round his temples to keep his emotions from flaring up as surely as the ill-fated crumpet.

He leaned against the windowsill, deep in thought, and gradually the evening breeze calmed his feelings and set his mind upon a track it had not travelled for a long time. It took him back seventeen years to the days when his voice was shriller, his hair thicker and his knees dirtier than they were now. Now he came to think of it, he must have been a rowdy little specimen himself in those days, and quite capable of behaving in the same idiotic way as Jennings and Darbishire... H'm! Perhaps he *had* been a bit hasty. After all, Margaret was a very good judge of these matters, and if she was so sure that the boys were the victims of an unfortunate accident, he was prepared to take her word for it. Especially as the alternative was the probability of seeing chatty childhood anecdotes about Lancelot Wilkins, Esq., in the *Form Three Times!*

He turned back from the window and said: "I don't want to be unfair, Margaret, so I'll tell you what I suggest: I'll just make them do the sums they missed this afternoon, without giving them a further punishment for missing them."

"That sounds fair enough," she replied, with all the reasonableness of a younger sister who has got her own way.

"And – er, you won't – er – " How should he put it? Mr Wilkins fumbled for the right words as he brought the conversation back to a delicate subject. "What I mean is, you won't say anything about Lancelot Phineas and all that apple tree nonsense, will you?"

"No," said Margaret, "provided you agree to be perfectly sweet to them when they come to explain their absence."

"*Perfectly sweet!*" echoed her brother in tones of outraged horror. "I... I... Corwumph!... Perfectly sweet, I ask you!" He sank into a chair, *corwumphing* softly and muttering "Perfectly sweet!" through clenched teeth. He groped feebly for the teapot on the table. He felt he badly needed a cup of strong tea.

It was not long before the patter of feet was heard on the landing and a whispered argument broke out beyond the door. The words were not clear, but the tones had the breathless tension of a debate that has reached a critical stage.

"Wss wss wss I vote wss wss Mr Wilkins wss wss wss," said the first whisperer.

"Bzz bzz bzz my father says bzz bzz bzz," answered the second.

After that came a shuffling of feet as though a drill squad was falling in and picking up its dressing from the right. Then, the knock at the door and the drill squad marched in – a sad faced column, one abreast and two deep.

"Please, sir, we've come to report to you, sir."

"Ah, yes, of course! Come in, Jennings and Darbishire," Mr Wilkins greeted them with the heartiness of a man determined to be perfectly sweet even though it killed him. "Well, well! I thought you might drop in to see me. You – er, you've met my sister, I believe."

He smiled and waved a hand in her direction, but neither of the boys felt equal to meeting her eye; so they mumbled polite throat noises and stared down at their shoes.

"I suppose you've called about the – the little informal class I arranged for this afternoon," Mr Wilkins went on with a sidelong glance to make sure that his sister was paying attention to his charm of manner. He was taking no chances where she was concerned!

Jennings found his voice. "We're most terribly sorry we were absent, sir, and for everything we said, too, sir."

"Ah, well, accidents will happen! Pity you missed it, though. We learned quite a lot."

The two boys couldn't believe their ears. What on earth was the matter with Mr Wilkins? They had arrived with nerves braced to withstand the shattering thunderbolts of his wrath, and lo and behold! they were being welcomed like film stars at a gathering of their fans! The thing just didn't make sense. Surely, by now, he must have heard a repeat programme of their ill-chosen comments! Why, then, they wondered, was he not towering with rage and tearing off strips left, right and centre?

"I think the best thing will be if you come and see me before you go to bed and we'll work through some of those examples together, shall we?"

"Yes, sir: willingly, sir. Thank you very much, sir." Darbishire wriggled his toes in embarrassed gratitude. And Jennings asked, with wonder in his voice: "But…is that *all*, sir?"

"Yes, that's all. Unless – oh, yes, have something to eat before you go."

Mr Wilkins was thorough: if he'd *got* to be perfectly sweet, he'd do the job so well that no criticism could be levelled at his perfect sweetness. He thrust the crumpet plate towards Jennings, who recoiled at the sight of food at such close quarters.

"Oh, no, really – thanks very much all the same, sir."

"Go on, boy – have a crumpet when I tell you to!"

"But, sir, I couldn't, sir."

"Nonsense!" said Mr Wilkins heartily. "Boys can always eat crumpets. Why I remember when I was your age – er, well, never mind – have a crumpet!"

They were saved by Margaret coming to their aid. "I shouldn't press them if I were you, *Mister* Wilkins," she advised. "I think they've had enough for one afternoon."

Mr Wilkins put the plate back on the table, and then stiffened suddenly as his sister went on: "By the way, Jennings, I was going to give you some suggestions for your magazine, wasn't I?"

"Well, yes, you *were*, Miss Wilkins. But after what I said, I thought – I mean – I didn't think…" His voice trailed off in guilty silence.

"But I should be only too pleased to help! Now let me see! What can I tell you about my brother that would make interesting reading!"

Mr Wilkins gripped the tablecloth in alarm. Surely she wasn't going back on her word after he had fulfilled his part of the bargain!

"Now, look here, Margaret, be fair! You distinctly promised…"

"Don't interrupt, dear, I'm trying to think… Oh, yes! Some years ago my brother…"

Pink with indignation, Mr Wilkins swung round and faced his sister. "Margaret... I... I... Corwumph! I won't have it; I forbid you to..."

But what was the use of protesting? Nothing short of physical violence could stem the flow of her harmful chatter. He stared at the speaker with unbelieving eyes. That his own sister, of whom he was so fond, should let him down after promising faithfully... He listened, numb with embarrassment, as she continued.

"Don't be so modest, Mr Wilkins! I'm sure you wouldn't mind their knowing this; some years ago, Jennings, when my brother was at the University, he rowed in the Cambridge crew that won the Boat Race three years running."

The words acted like magic. Jennings and Darbishire skipped up and down, flapping their fingers with delight.

"Golly, did he really! How supersonic; I say, congratulations, sir!"

"Wacko! What super-cracking, jet-propelled news! May I shake hands with you, sir?"

The magic spell worked more slowly on Mr Wilkins; but when he had recovered from the shock, he stood pleased and beaming, and uncertain what to say.

"Oh, sir, this is wonderful news, sir. Fancy you being a famous oarsman, sir! Why didn't you ever tell us before, sir?"

"Well – I – er... Doesn't do to blow your own trumpet," said Mr Wilkins, and blew his nose instead to cover his embarrassment.

There was no reason, of course, why his distinguished athletic record should not be known, but it was hardly the sort of thing that a modest man could have revealed himself. Now that his sister had done it for him, he glowed with a quiet pride and felt absurdly shy.

"You shouldn't have told them, Margaret," he said, with good-humoured reproof which suggested that he would have been disappointed if she *hadn't*.

"You're not so unfamous as we thought, sir," said Darbishire, his eyes shining triumphantly behind his spectacles. "Why, you'll be the hero of the school when the *Form Three Times* comes out."

"I'm quite sure you don't want to fill up your paper with unimportant things like that," said Mr Wilkins modestly.

"Oh, but we *do*, sir! It's just the sort of thing we need. We may print it, mayn't we, sir?" Jennings begged. "And I'd like to take a photo of you and put that in. It'd look ever so smashing on the front page: *Mr L P Wilkins, the famous rowing Blue*." And then, carried away by the excitement of the moment, he asked: "What does LP stand for, sir? We really ought to put your full name in to round it off nicely, don't you think, sir."

It was an unfortunate question, and for a second it seemed that the joyful atmosphere might dissolve in a sudden squall of disapproval.

Tactfully, Margaret saved the situation. "In athletic circles, Jennings, my brother was always known by his initials, so it will be quite correct to describe him as L P Wilkins, Esq."

Satisfied, the boys took their leave and bounded out through the door in happy contrast to their recent dismal entrance. But a moment later, Jennings was back.

"Please, Miss Wilkins, I quite forgot to tell you about that fifty pence we owe," he said. "Venables won't agree to pay, because he says we went over the limit, but if you wouldn't mind waiting, Darbishire and I could send you five pence a week for ten weeks."

"That's all right, Jennings; you can forget about it. In any case, you agreed I was to be a *paying* guest," she said.

"Oh, but really, we couldn't possibly let you…"

Miss Margaret Wilkins rose from her chair and stood with shoulders squared, the light of battle gleaming in her eye. For the first time, Jennings noticed a faint family resemblance to her brother, which became more marked as she announced in firm tones: "You may or may not know, Jennings, that the Wilkins family can be very severe when they like. If you argue with them they become fire-breathing dragons of the most frantic type. So if you don't stop talking nonsense about that fifty pence, I shall – " she sought in her mind for the right expression – "I shall get in a supersonic bate and explode!"

"Yes, Miss Wilkins, thank you, Miss Wilkins," said Jennings meekly, and tiptoed out and closed the door.

17

Here is the News!

At a table in a corner of the hobbies room sat the editors of the *Form Three Times*. Their brows were furrowed in thought and their teeth bit deeply into the pencils rooted between their jaws; for it was Monday evening and zero hour was almost upon them, when Mr Carter would be ready to tap their pencilled paragraphs into neat typescript.

They had been careful to allow no leakage of the news about Mr Wilkins' fame as an oarsman, which they were planning to spring upon their readers as a sensational surprise. It had not been easy to keep the topic to themselves, when all over the weekend they had been bursting to tell everyone they met. But they had kept their secret even in the face of direct questions.

"What happened when you reported to Old Wilkie?" Venables had asked at breakfast on Sunday morning.

"Nothing much. He went through the sums with us before the dorm. bell last night," Jennings had answered.

"Yes, but before that – what sort of punishment did he dole out?"

"Well, he *was* going to make us eat a crumpet, but he let us off." It was a mystifying reply, but Jennings refused to enlarge upon it.

Now, however, the time had come to put the finishing touches to their exclusive story and the editors were determined to make a success of it.

"We ought to do a big mauve headline on the printing outfit," said Jennings. "*L P Wilkins, Esq., is an old…*"

"Gosh, be careful, Jen! We called him enough names to be going on with on Saturday afternoon," Darbishire cautioned.

"No, I was going to say *L P Wilkins, Esq., is an old Cambridge Blue.* That's quite a decent thing to say about anyone. In fact I'd never have said all those others if I'd known before. It sort of puts a chap in a different light if you know he's rowed in the Boat Race, doesn't it!"

Darbishire nodded his agreement. "He was quite human when I had a chat with him about it after chapel yesterday. He says you have to be as keen as a beaver if you want to get picked for the crew. He and another chap used to get up early and practise every morning."

"Perhaps that'd be a good way to start off our chatty paragraph, then. Something like: *When Mr Wilkins was young he always used to have a row with someone before breakfast.*"

Jennings wrote it down, and then grinned as the double meaning dawned on him. "Goodness, we can't say that, Darbi! There's two ways of pronouncing *r-o-w* and it sounds as though he was always kicking up a hoo-hah."

"That wouldn't surprise me, either – knowing Old Wilkie," said Darbishire. "Still, it might be better to say that when he went *rowing* he always used a boat, so chaps won't jump to the wrong conclusion."

"But that's stark, raving crackers! Of *course* you'd go rowing in a boat – where else?"

It was these stumbling blocks in the path of English composition which delayed their work and accounted for the furrows on their foreheads. They tried many ways of making their meaning clear: they put Mr Wilkins in a boat, in brackets; they added a footnote that the words *row, rowing, rowed*, must be rhymed with *flow, flowing, flowed*, and not with *vow, vowing, vowed*. They even tried to avoid using the word altogether and wrote that L P Wilkins, Esq., was famed for his Oxford and Cambridge boat-racemanship.

And finally, they crossed most of it out and took their notebook to Mr Carter whose brow also became furrowed as he struggled to read the manuscript. But after careful revision he was able to tap the paragraphs into some semblance of order on his typewriter.

Jennings and Darbishire went upstairs to bed in a state of pent-up excitement. Soon their closely-guarded secret would be common property; Mr Wilkins would be acclaimed a hero and the editors of the *Form Three Times* could bask in the reflected glory of the light which he had hidden for so long under a bushel.

"I can't get over Old Wilkie being a famous sportsman," mused Darbishire, absently stretching his garter onto his head like a tight-fitting halo. "It's a good job we found out, because his life-story needed livening up a bit. We're like these old historian geezers discovering new facts about the life of Oliver Cromwell."

"Except that it didn't happen as long ago as all that," Jennings reminded him. "It's Mr Carter who's so old you have to work it out by algebra. I got him to tell me that sum again, but I couldn't work it out with x's and y's so I used a's and b's instead."

"And what's the answer?"

"Well, it's just possible I made a bish somewhere, because according to my figures he must have been a hundred-and-six last birthday. It just shows you can't believe everything grown-ups say."

"It's the way their minds work when they get old," Darbishire assured him. "You just can't tell what they're going to do next. Look at Old Wilkie last Saturday: there we were quaking and shivering with nerves at the thought of him going off like a depth-charge, and ten seconds later our nerves were shaking and quivering with surprise because he never exploded at all!"

"Never mind; there'll be an explosion all right, tomorrow, when the chaps find out that our jet-propelled fire-breathing dragon is really a famous sporting character in disguise. Just as well we can prove it, because no one would ever think he was a sheep in wolf's clothing, to look at him – would they!"

Jennings' prophecy proved correct. The *Form Three Times* appeared on the common room noticeboard at break the next morning, and everybody was so busy discussing the sensational news on page one, that they had no time to spare for reading the rest of the paper.

This was a pity, for there were some interesting items for the student of current affairs: page two offered an account of the 2nd XI match against Bracebridge and a thrilling story of how two members of the visiting party had stumbled upon the remainder, whom they found benighted on the treacherous grassy slopes of Pottlewhistle. On page three were Gardening Notes by *Our Horticultural Correspondent* and some hints on *How to Play Football*, written – but wisely not signed – by C E J Darbishire.

The winner of the handwriting competition could have seen his name, in block capitals on page four; and here, also, the unsuccessful poets were highly commended in smaller type. A new *Life of O Cromwell* on page five might have proved useful to any serious student of history; and those who favoured hobbies of a practical sort could have enjoyed an article on

Cooking and Photography, by J C T Jennings, in which the author stressed the importance of doing only one of these things at a time.

But in spite of this rich offering, the eyes of the readers remained fixed on page one, where their minds were stirred by the story of three historic Boat Races in which L P Wilkins, Esq., had been a prominent member of the Cambridge crew.

And after they had read it, a change of heart came upon them and they went about telling everyone they met what a decent chap Old Wilkie was, and how they had always liked him really, only they'd never thought of saying so before.

Mr Wilkins signed two dozen autograph books that morning, and then shut himself in his room and refused to answer the door. He avoided looking at the noticeboard for three days, but on the evening of the fourth, after the boys were safely in bed, Mr Carter met him tiptoeing furtively away from the common room door.

Casually he inquired: "Well, Wilkins, what do you think of your biography?"

"Silly little boys!" replied Mr Wilkins. "If only they'd show as much interest in their algebra as they do in the Boat Race we might be getting somewhere. *Silly* little boys!"

But it was clear from his tone that he was really rather pleased.

Next day, the Headmaster honoured the common room with one of his rare visits. The editors were there and watched from a polite distance as he stood and read the magazine from end to end.

"I wonder what he thinks of it!" whispered Darbishire.

"You can never tell with the Archbeako," Jennings whispered back. "He's got one of those faces that don't light up very much."

Something, however, must have registered, because Mr Pemberton-Oakes strolled over and had a word with Mr Carter, who was supervising the common room activities; and from their glances at the noticeboard it was obvious what the two men were talking about. As soon as the Head had gone, Jennings and Darbishire made a bee-line for the duty master.

"Sir, please sir, what did he say, sir?"

"Yes, sir; did he like it, sir?"

"I think so," Mr Carter replied. "He told me he approves of creative hobbies of this kind, because as well as being valuable in themselves, they keep you out of mischief."

"Oh, wacko! That's jolly high praise, isn't it. sir! We thought he'd be pleased with all the culture and stuff, because Darbishire says that his father says…"

Jennings stopped, puzzled by the quiet smile which had appeared at the corners of Mr Carter's mouth, as though he was deep in the enjoyment of some private joke.

"What's the matter, sir? Have I said something funny?"

"No, no," said Mr Carter hastily. "I was just smiling at the idea of the *Form Three Times* keeping you out of mischief."

"Why, what do you mean, sir?" asked Darbishire.

Mr Carter thought for a moment. Then he said: "Well, during the last few weeks, some odd things have come to my notice. I remember hearing of queer developments in the dark room and an unexpected obstruction in a chimney which occurred after you had returned from a journalistic expedition bearing a parcel of fish. I put two and two together – and decided not to inquire into the matter too deeply!"

The faces of his audience showed that they agreed with the wisdom of this decision.

"I remember, also, a sudden interest in Latin books that the Headmaster happened to mention," Mr Carter went on. "I'm not quite sure what was behind it all, but I *do* know that when we arranged to hold a text-book inspection at short notice it caused quite a stir throughout Form Three."

"Yes, sir… Sorry, sir. I didn't know you knew all that, sir," Jennings mumbled. The conversation was taking an awkward turn. Was Mr Carter preparing for action?

Jennings needn't have worried. Mr Carter's private detective service was efficient, but he seldom interfered unless matters threatened to get out of hand. The master was still wearing his quiet smile as he turned to leave the room: at the door he paused.

"Don't look so baffled, Jennings," he said. "I think the *Form Three Times* is an excellent paper and well worth doing. And, what's more, I've every reason to be grateful to this – er, creative hobby of yours for keeping you out of even worse mischief!"

The editors exchanged glances as the door closed, and Darbishire heaved a sigh of relief,

"Well, fossilised fish-hooks! Fancy him guessing all that!" he murmured. "I've always said that's the one snag about Mr Carter – he finds out simply *everything*."

"You don't have to tell *me* that," the chief editor answered. "But he's pretty decent the way he never gets in a bate about it and kicks up hoo-hahs: not like *some* people I could mention, even if they did row in the Boat Race!"

Jennings grinned as his mind travelled back over the misfortunes of the past few weeks. He looked up and saw that Darbishire was grinning too, and a moment later both grins broke into peals of laughter.

They felt pleased and proud and light-hearted; the *Form Three Times* had been well worth every bit of their trouble. Admittedly, it had given them some anxious moments, but now that these were safely behind them, they could see the funny side of things. And, after all, what more could anyone want than that!

ANTHONY BUCKERIDGE

ACCORDING TO JENNINGS

Super-whacko wheeze!

'There you are! How about that for a space-helmet!' cried Jennings triumphantly.

'Jolly good: fits like a glove,' was Darbishire's verdict.
'Attention, all space shipping!' Jennings announced in ringing tones. 'Here comes the one-and-only famous Butch Breakaway, touching down on the moon in his supersonic radio-controlled space-helmet...'

The boys at Linbury Court Preparatory School are eager to speed up the progress of space travel, and none more so than Jennings, whose first task is to find a suitable helmet. But is it really a good idea to take a dome-shaped glass-case, which previously housed a stuffed woodpecker, and place it over his head?

Petrified paintpots!

Jennings and Darbishire's luck is in when they hitch a ride with an international cricketer, and could it be that they've done something right for once when they attempt to apprehend a suspected burglar?

Bat-witted clodpoll!

ANTHONY BUCKERIDGE

JENNINGS' DIARY

Hah-ooh cinosrepus!

'*Selbanev, Nosnikta, Senoj-Nitram*,' said Jennings. 'They're the names of people, I bet you can't guess who!'

'Russian agents?... Zulu tribesmen?... Ancient kings of Egypt?' hazarded Darbishire.

'No, no, no,' Jennings flipped his fingers in delight and danced ungainly ballet steps round the tuck-boxes. 'Oh, wacko! If you can't guess, neither will anybody else, so we can use it for the code.'

Jennings is suffering from beginning-of-term-itis, but things soon return to the normal state of mayhem and confusion when his new diary is made public property! Alarmed at the thought of his most private thoughts being made public, Jennings decides to invent a secret language. Will anyone be able to decode *Selbanev si a llopdolc*?

Drazo Hsivips!

Inspired by a visit to the Natural History Museum, Jennings and Darbishire establish their own collection of ancient relics, but they are not out of trouble for long and when the precious diary goes missing, Jennings finds himself on the wrong side of the law!

Relggowsnroh emoseurg!

ANTHONY BUCKERIDGE

JENNINGS FOLLOWS A CLUE

Fossilized fish-hooks!

'We must have a headquarters, where we can meet and work out clues and things. We might even put up a notice so that chaps will know where to come when they want mysteries solved. Something like *Linbury Court Detective Agency – Chief Investigator, J C T Jennings…*'

When Jennings is inspired to take up a career as a detective, with faithful Darbishire as his assistant, trouble is bound to be just around the corner. Their first mission – to recover a 'stolen' sports cup, is the first of several bungled attempts to imitate super sleuth Sherlock Holmes.

Frightful bish!

But the detective duo face their most perilous adventure yet when they make a nocturnal visit to the sanatorium and discover that they are not alone. An intruder is at large, but a missing coat button is Jennings' only clue.

Crystallised cheesecakes!

ANTHONY BUCKERIDGE

JENNINGS GOES TO SCHOOL

Smash-on prang!

'That shepherd's pie we've just had was supersonic muck so it's wizard, but this school jam's ghastly so it's ozard…being a new chap's pretty ozard for a bit, but you'll get used to it when you've been here as long as I have.'

When Jennings arrives at Linbury Court Preparatory School as a new boy, he soon discovers how much he has to learn, especially when the other boys seem to be talking in a different language!

Spivish ozard!

But it is not long before Jennings becomes a celebrity, following an intrepid escape from the school grounds and a riotous attempt to enliven a fire-practice, which leaves Old Wilkie literally climbing the walls! From then on, every time Jennings gives trouble the elbow, a new disaster trips him over. But only one thing really matters to J C T Jennings – his First Eleven debut. When the long-awaited match arrives, Jennings certainly uses his head.

Super-duper breezy!

Anthony Buckeridge

Jennings' Little Hut

Supersonic hoo-hah!

Jennings and Darbishire watched with mounting horror. Earthquakes and landslides seemed to be happening before their eyes. The little hut was heaving like a thing possessed. 'Oh, fish-hooks!' breathed Jennings in dismay. 'He's smashing up the place like a bulldozer!'

The woodland at Linbury Court becomes squatters' territory when Jennings comes up with the idea of building huts out of reeds and branches. Jennings and Darbishire are thrilled with their construction, which even includes a patented prefabricated ventilating shaft, a special irrigation drainage canal and a pontoon suspension bridge!

Gruesome hornswoggler!

But things can only go horribly wrong for Jennings when he is put in charge of Elmer, the treasured goldfish, and even worse when the headmaster pays the squatters a visit. And if Jennings thinks that a game of cricket will be far less trouble, he's going to be knocked for six!

Rotten chizzler!